EGYPTIAN MYTHOLOGY

Classic Stories of Egyptian Myths, Gods, Goddesses,
Heroes, and Monsters, The Prince and The
Sphinx,Greek Princess

Roberts Parizi

TABLE OF CONTENTS

Introduction

First off, I would like to thank you for choosing this book. I hope that whether you choose it for purely entertainment purposes or a learning experience, that it does just that.

This book is filled with Egyptian myths and folktales that will teach you a bit about their culture and keep you entertained for hours. Egyptian mythology tends to pale in comparison to Greek or Norse mythology, but their stories and history is just as exciting. I'm glad you have found yourself here, though, as Egyptian mythology is so unique and diverse.

If you are familiar with any of their myths, there is a good chance you may find that some of these stories are slightly different. That's because over the years, the stories have been changed, by accident, during their numerous retelling and translations. The stories can also sometimes differ depending on the region of Egypt they came from.

Before we get into the stories, though, we will cover the history of Egyptian mythology, along with the gods and goddesses, and role the mythology plays in Egypt.

One last thing before we begin, if you find any part of this book helpful or entertaining, I ask that you please leave a review.

Chapter 1: The History of Egyptian Mythology

Egyptian mythology is a belief structure and a type of ancient Egyptian culture that has been around since about 4000 BCE. You can find evidence about this by paintings in tombs and their burial practices. This ancient culture was around until Cleopatra VII died in 30 BCE. She was the last ruler of Egypt's Ptolemaic Dynasty. All the aspects of ancient Egyptian life were created from stories related to the world's creation, and the gods were sustaining that world.

Egypt's religion went on to influence other cultures by transmitting them through their trade routes. They became extremely widespread after they opened the Silk Road in 130 BCE since the city of Alexandria was one of their most important commercial centers. Egyptian mythology had a huge significance on other cultures because of its development about the concept of a person having eternal life after they die, reincarnation, and benevolent deities. The Egyptian belief of reincarnation influenced both Plato and Pythagoras from Greece. The Romans borrowed this from Egypt, along with other civilizations.

The existence of humans was understood to be just a small part of their eternal journey. Their lives were presided over and orchestrated by forces that took form as various deities that made up the Egyptian pantheon. The historian Bunson states:

"Heh, called Huh in some eras, was one of the original gods of the Ogdoad, which are the eight deities worshipped during the Old Kingdom between 2575 to 2134 BCE, at Hermopolis and represented eternity. The goal and destiny of all human life in Egyptian religious beliefs, a stage of existence in which mortals could attain everlasting bliss."

A person's life on Earth wasn't just a prologue to something better but was once part of the person's whole journey. Their concept of an afterlife was a "mirror-world" to their own life, and a person should live their life if they want to enjoy their eternal journey.

The World's Creation

For the Egyptians, their journey started when the world and universe were created from swirling dark chaos. At one time, there wasn't anything but endless water that was dark without the form's purpose. Heka existed inside this void. He was the god of magic. He was waiting for the moment to create something. Out of the silence rose a hill that is known as the ben-ben.

On top of that hill stood the god Atum. Atum looked out at all this nothingness and saw that he was alone, and by the use of his magic, he mated with his shadow and gave birth to two children. Tefnut, the goddess of moisture, Atum vomited out while he spat out Shu, who is the god of air. She gave to the world all of life's principles, and Tefnut contributed to the order of those principles.

They left their father on the ben-ben, and they went to establish the world. At some time, Atum started worrying because his children had been gone so long, and he removed his eye and sent it out to search for them. While his eye was on its little journey, Atum sat alone on his hill in the middle of all this chaos and thought about eternity. Tefnut and Shu came back with his eye, and since their father was so grateful for the safe return, he shed tears of joy. Those tears dropped on to the dark earth of ben-ben and gave birth to women and men. His eye became known as the All-Seeing Eye, Eye of Ra, or the Udjat eye.

These people didn't have anywhere to live, and so Tefnut and Shu mated and had the children of Nut, the sky, and Geb, the earth. Nut and Geb, even though they were sister and brother, fell in love with each other and could not be separated. Atum found this behavior to be unacceptable and pushed them apart. He moved Nut high up in the heavens. These two lovers could always see each other but could not touch each other anymore. Nut was already with child and gave birth to Horus, Nephthys, Set, Isis, and Osiris. These are the five Egyptian gods that are most recognized as the most important and familiar representation of the older god-figures. Osiris showed himself to be a judicious and thoughtful god and was given the world to rule by Atum. Atum then went off an attended his own affairs.

Set and Osiris

Osiris helped the world effectively. He co-ruled with Isis, his sister-wife. He decided where the trees would grow best, and the water flowed very sweetly. He created the Nile River and Egypt to provide for all the people's needs.

In everything, he acted in accordance with harmony and honored his siblings and father by keeping everything in balance. Set, his brother, was envious of this creation and of Osiris' glory and power. He had his brother's measurements taken secretly and ordered an elaborate chest to be made to those specifications. Once the chest was finished, Set threw a huge banquet, and he invited Osiris and 72 other people. When the party ended, he offered the chest as a gift to anyone who could fit inside. Of course, Osiris fit perfectly. When he was comfortable inside the coffin, Set slammed the lid shut and threw it into the Nile. He then made up a story that Osiris was dead and took overruling the world.

Isis didn't believe that her husband was really dead and decided to search for him. She finally found the coffin inside of a tree at Byblos. The people who lived here were pleased to help her get the coffin out of the tree. For their help, Isis blessed them. They later became the main exporters of papyrus. Some people think that this detail was added later by scribes to honor the city that was so important to this person's trade. Isis brought Osiris' body back to Egypt and started gathering herbs to make potions that could bring Osiris back to life. She left Nephthys, her sister, to guard the place where she hid his body.

All this time, Set was worried that Isis might find Osiris' body and figure out a way to bring him back to life because she was very knowledgeable and powerful about these things. When Set found Isis gone, he asked Nephthys where she had gone, and when the goddess answered, he knew she was lying. He could get Nephthys to tell him where Osiris' body was and immediately went there. He tore the coffin open, and he cut the body into 42 pieces, even though some people say it was only 14. He then threw all Osiris' body parts all over Egypt's land so that Isis wouldn't ever be able to find them, and once this was accomplished, he went back to his palace to rule.

Once Isis returned and saw that the coffin had been destroyed and Osiris' body gone, she fell on her knees in deep despair and cried uncontrollably. Nephthys felt guilty because she had betrayed Isis' secret and told her what had happened and helped her find all of Osiris' parts. The sisters started searching for Osiris' parts. Anywhere they found a body part, they would bury it where it lay and built a shrine to protect it from Set. By doing this, the 42 provinces of Egypt were created by these two goddesses.

They had finally assembled all of his body except his penis. A fish had eaten this. Isis created a replacement part for his penis and mated with her husband. She became pregnant with Horus, their son. Isis had successfully brought Osiris back to life, but since he wasn't whole, he couldn't rule lie he had before. He descended into the underworld to become the ruler and judge of the land of the dead.

To differentiate him from his uncle Horus was known as Horus the Younger, their child Horus was brought up in secret to protect him from Set. Once he grew into manhood, he challenged his uncle to be the ruler of his father's kingdom. The battle went on for 80 years until Horus finally defeated Set and banished him from Egypt to dwell in the deserts. Horus then ruled with Isis, his mother, and Nephthys, his aunt. They became his counselors, and once again, harmony was restored to their land.

Ma'at's Importance

Even though there are many variations of this myth, the one element that remains the same in all of them is harmony, and anytime it gets disrupted, it has to be restored. The main principle of ma'at was always in the center of every myth and their mythology, in some form or other. It relies on this value to give it the information. One historian, Jill Kamil, states: "Storytelling played an important part in the ancient Egyptian's lives. The deeds of their kings and gods weren't written down in the early times, and they only found their way through oral translations into the literature at a later date." It is interesting to see that no matter what generation these tales were from, harmonious balance or ma'at is at the heart of all of them.

Everything within the universe was thought to be kept in constant balance without an ending, and since humans were part of this universe, they participated in this balance. Ma'at was possible by an underlying force that existed before creation and made every aspect of life possible, and that force was heka. Heka was the power that allowed all the gods to do their duties while sustaining all life. This was personified by the god Heka who let a person's soul pass from this earthly existence into the afterlife.

When a person's soul leaves their body when they die, they thought it would appear in the Hall of Truth to stand before Osiris to be judged. The deceased person's heart would be weighed on a scale against Ma'at's white feather. If their heart was lighter than the feather, their soul was allowed to move into the Field of Reeds. This is the place of eternal bliss and purification. If their heart was more massive, it was dropped on the floor where Ammut, the monster, would eat it. Their soul would cease to exist.

Even though there was a concept of an underworld, there wasn't a "hell" as most people understand them to be in all the modern monotheistic relations. As Bunson states: "The Egyptians were afraid of eternal darkness and unconsciousness in the afterlife because both conditions belied the orderly transmission of light and movement evident in the universe." Since existence was one more part of their universal journey that begins with Atum and the ben-ben, it was the soul's natural state. Just thinking about being separated from that journey of not existing was more terrifying than any torment they might experience in the underworld. A person still existed in the land of eternal pain.

One concept of an underworld that is similar to "hell" that the Christians believe in did develop in Egypt but wasn't accepted universally. Bunson states: "Eternity was the common destination of each man, woman, and child in Egypt. Such a belief infused the vision of the people, and gave them a certain vitality for life un-matched anywhere in the ancient world." The Ancient Egyptians' mythology reflected this joy in living. It also inspired the great monuments and temples that are a huge part of Egypt's legacy. The admiration of Egyptian mythology and its culture is a testimony to the power of the life-affirming message that can be seen in these ancient tales.

Chapter 2: Egyptian Gods and Goddesses

Ancient Egypt was a land that was alive with the spirits of their gods. Their sun god, Ra, would get rid of the darkness each morning while riding in his boat. He would bring light. Other gods would watch over Egypt's people at night like stars. Osiris would cause the Nile River to flood so it could fertilize the land while the god Khnum directed where it flowed. Isis and her sister Nephthys would walk with the people in their daily lives and protected them when they died. They had the help of other gods, too. Bastet guarded women and watched over their homes. Tennent, the goddess of brewing and beer, would also be with women during childbirth. Hathor held a lot of roles. She would always be close by at any festival or party and was known as the Lady of Darkness.

These goddesses and gods were not deities to be afraid of, but they were close friends who lived with the people. They were always present at the shrines that the people built for them in the swamps, streams, lakes, trees, and in the deserts beyond the Nile. Anytime the hot winds would blow in, it wasn't just junction of air but Set causing trouble. Anytime the rains fell, it was looked at as a gift from Tefnut, the goddess known as *She of Moisture*. She is also associated with dryness and would be asked to hold back rain on any of their festival days. Humans were created from Atum's tears when he cried with joy when Tefnut and Shu, his children, returned at the beginning when the world was created out of chaos. In every aspect of life, Egypt's deities were present and continue to care for their people even after death.

Deities and Their Origins

People believing in supernatural entities have been around since the Predynastic Period, which was between 6000 and 3150 BCE. This practice is a lot older than this. Margaret Bunson, the historian, states: "The Egyptians lived with forces that they didn't understand. Floods, earthquakes, storms, and periods of drought seem inexplicable, yet the people realized acutely that natural forces impacted human affairs. The spirits of nature were thus deemed powerful because of the damage they could inflict on humans."

This early belief in gods did take on the forms of animals. They believed that objects that are inanimate like the earth, animals, plants, and objects all have souls and have a divine spark deep inside them. They had other beliefs, too. The belief of fetishism believed that all objects had supernatural powers and consciousness. Totemism was the belief that clans or individual people can have a spiritual relationship with specific symbols, animals, or plants. During the Predynastic Period, animism was the main way they understood the universe, just like all early people from any culture. By using animism, humans tried to explain all the forces of nature and how humans were part of this life on earth. Animism didn't just deal with higher universal forces and the energy of the earth but also the souls of the people who had died. To help explain this, Bunson says:

"The Egyptians believed firmly that death was just a doorway to another form of existence, so they acknowledged the possibility that those who had died were more powerful in their resurrected state. Thus politically, spiritually, or magically powerful members of each community took on special significance in death or in the realm beyond the grave. Special care was taken to provide these souls with all the reverence, offerings, and honors that were due to them. Dead people were thought to be able to involve themselves in the affairs of the living, for good or ill, and thus had to be placated with daily sacrifices."

Believing in life after death gave awareness to understanding of supernatural beings who watched over this realm and other realms that connected them to the earthly plane. The early creation of religious beliefs could best be summed up by a line from Emily Dickinson's poem *My Life Closed Twice Before its Close*: "Parting is all we know of heaven" or from Larkin's *Aubade* that states religion was "created to pretend we never die." Experiencing death takes some explanations and meanings that were provided by believing in higher powers.

Animisn branched into totemism and fetishism. Totemism grew out of the local association with certain animals or plants. All provinces of ancient Egypt had a totem that was unique to them. Some might have been just a symbol, animal, or plant that showed the people's connection to the spirits at that location. Fetishism is illustrated by the symbol of the "djed," as it represents cosmic and earthly stability. This symbol was thought to have been a fertility sign at one time that was associated with Osiris so that there were some inscriptions that said "the Djed is laid on its side" meant that Osiris had died. If the djed was upright it meant they had been resurrected. Every one of the Egyptian's armies marched into battle. These armies had been divided into nomes. Within each nome, the people carried their own staff that flew its totem. People could have their own totem, too that allowed their spirit guides to watch over them. Every king of Egypt would have their own hawk that watched over them. This hawk always represented Horus.

With time, the spirits that were known by animism became more human like. These invisible spirits that lived in the universe were given a shape, form, and name. These became ancient Egypt's deities.

Origins of Mythology

The main creation myth starts with the stillness of the waters before time began. From these endless depths, rose a mound known as ben-ben. It is said that they pyramids in Egypt were created to show the first hill on earth that rose out of this primordial depth. Existing outside of these water or Nu was an entity called Heka or magic. This became known as the god Heka. In some versions of this myth, Heka caused ben-ben to rise.

On top of this mound stood Atum or sometimes known as Ra. He comes to ben-ben from the air. He looked out on all the nothingness and realized he was alone. Through Heka, he mated with his shadow and gave birth to two children. Atum spat out Shu or the god of air. He then vomited out Tefnut or the goddess of moisture. Shu gave the world all the principles of life while Tefnut worked with the principles of order.

They left Atum on top of ben-ben and went to establish the world. With some time, Atum got worried about his children and he took his eye out to sent it out to search for them. During the time his eye was gone, he sat alone on ben-ben in the middle of all the chaos and thought about eternity. Tefnut and Shu returned to their father with his eye. This became known as the "All-Seeing Eye." Since their father was grateful that they returned safely, he shed joyful tears.

These tears dropped onto the dark earth and gave birth to women and men. these people didn't have anywhere to live so Tefnut and Shu mated and gave birth to the earth (Geb) and the sky (Nut) who fell in love with each other so much that they became inseparable. Atum was not at all pleased with this and he pushed them away from each other. He put Nut far above Geb and fastened her to the cosmos. Geb was already pregnant at the time of their separation and she gave birth to five gods: Horus, Nephthys, Set, Isis, and Osiris. From all of these first gods others were born.

Another version of this is similar but it involves Neith, the goddess, which is one of Egypt's oldest deities. In this version, Neith is Nu's wife. Nu is the primordial chaos that births Atum and the other gods. Heka still outdates Neith and all the other gods. In several telling of Egypt's history, Neith is called the "Mother of the Gods" or "Mother of All." She is the earliest example of a Mother Goddess in history. In another version, Nu or the chaos is given the personification of Nun. These were the mother and father of every creartion who births all the goddesses and gods an all other things within the universe.

Geraldine Pinch, an Egyptologist, says that after the gods were born and creation was set into motion:

"Qualities of the primeval state, such as its darkness, were retrospectively endowed with consciousness and became a group of deities know asn the Eight or the Ogdoad of Hermopolis. The Eight were imagined as amphibians and reptiles, fertile creatures of the dark primeval slime. They were the forces that shaped the creator or even the first manifestations of the creator."

The symbol of the snake swallowing its tail or ouroborus, represents eternity. This comes from their connection to the serpent, creation, and the divine. Atum or Ra is shown in their early inscriptions as a serpent. Later on, he became the sun deity that was protected by a serpent who fights the chaos and is symbolized by Apophis, the serpent.

The Goddesses' and Gods' Nature

Ancient Egypt's deities kept that balance and harmony once the primordial One was divided at creation. Geraldine Pinch states: "Texts that allude to the unknowable era before creation define it as the time before two things had developed. The cosmos was not yet divided into pairs of opposites such as earth and sky, light and darkness, male and female, or life and death." In the beginning, everything was One and when ben-ben rose and all the gods were birthed and multi deities entering into creation. The One then became many.

The Egyptian's beliefs centered on balancing all these "many" through a principle of harmony that was known as Ma'at. These became the central value in the Egyptian culture that influenced all aspects of a person's lives from the way they conducted themselves and on into their literature, architecture, art, and even how they viewed their afterlife. The power that allowed the gods to do their jobs, allowed the humans to access their gods, and sustained Heka and Ma'at. Heka is said to have existed before any other gods.

Some scholars claim that the Egyptians developed their religious beliefs just like the people from Mesopotamia. Egyptians thought they were partners with all the gods to help keep order and holding chaos at bay. The story that bests illustrate this concept is *The Overthrowing of Apophis* that created a ritual of its own. Apophis is the serpent who attacks Ra's barge as it travels through the darkness. Various goddesses and gods would ride on the boat with Ra to protect him from Apophis. All the dead souls were expected to help fight the serpent. The most famous image shows Set, the god, spearing the serpent to protect the light. This was before Set became known as a villain in the Osiris Myth.

The ritual that grew from this story included people that made images of Apophis from wax or wood and then destroyed them in a fire to help all the dead souls along with the deities that traveled with them to help the sun come up each morning. Days that were cloudy were worrisome for the ancient Egyptians since they took this as a sign that Apophis had overpowered Ra. The biggest scare was a solar eclipse. through their devotion to their gods and with rituals, they helped the sun come up each morning and every day was seen as a struggle between the forces of chaos and order.

Pinch states: "When creator gods such as Atum are spoken of a serpents they usually represent the positive aspect of chaos as an energy force but they had a negative counterpart in the great serpent Apophis. Apophis represented the destructive aspect of chaos that constantly tried to overwhelm all individual beings and reduce everything back to its primeval state of oneness. So, even before creation began, the world contained the elements of its own destruction."

This kind of destruction would overwhelm the goddesses and gods. In order to return the state back to normal all the goddesses and gods would combine forces with the One, was inevitable. Notable scholar Wilkinson, notes that many Egyptian texts show that even though the gods weren't thought of as mortal but they could die. this belief seems to come from their values of harmony and balance. Since all the gods in the universe had come from the One, it would go back to its original state at some time. Any god could be killed and then come back to life but since this was just a temporary situation, they believed that one day everyone would be put back into that primordial chaos from where they had come from.

Wilkinson states: "The principle of divine demise applies, in fact, to all Egyptian deities. Texts that date back to at least the New Kingdom tell of the god Thoth assigning fixed life spans to humans and gods alike, and Spell number 154 in the *Book of the Dead* unequivocally states that death or literally decay and disappearance awaits every god and goddess and only the elements from which the primordial world had arise would eventually remain."

Their concept of oneness wasn't valued by the Egyptians like it was with the Hindu or Chinese culture but is was feared. To go back to an undifferentiated oneness meant they had to lose their loved ones, their accomplishments, their memories, and their identity. the Egyptians could not tolerate these thoughts. They didn't believe in a "hell" but an afterlife. The worst thing that might happen to their soul was it being judged not fit to go into paradise. Once the heart of their soul was weighed against the feather of truth and was heavier than the feather, it got dropped onto the floor and eaten by Ammut, the monster.

Their heart was thought to be the center of their spirit and personality. When it was eaten by this monster, the soul no longer existed. Not being able to exist terrified them. Bunson states: "The Egyptians feared eternal darkness and unconsciousness in the afterlife because both conditions belied the orderly transmission of light and movement evident in the universe." This transmission of movement and light was life. Their vision of afterlife was the perfect reflection of their life on earth. It was created precisely due to their fear of not existing or of losing one's' self. When a god finally died, after about a million years, humans would die with them all and of history would not mean anything.

The Death of the Goddesses and Gods

The goddesses and gods on ancient Egypt did die eventually and it didn't take a million years. When Christiany rose, it meant the end of their ancient religious practices and a world that was sustained and full of magic. God lived in heaven. He was just one single deity that lived far away from the earth. There weren't all the different gods, goddesses, and spirits that inhabited their lives daily. Although this new God was present through his son, Jesus, he was still described as "dwelling in light inaccessible."

The Jews had taken the serpent and turned it into a symbol of human's being sent away from paradise. The earth was not longer full of spirits of friendly gods was thought to be evil and under the control of Satan. By the fifth century CE, the Egyptian gods began dwindling. By the seventh century CE, they had all disappeared. Wilkinson states that they didn't go quietly:

"In 383 AD, pagan temples throughout the Roman Empire were all closed by order from the Emperor Theodosius and a number of further decrees, culminating in those of Theodosius in 391 Ad and Valentinian III in 435 AD, sanctioned the actual destruction of pagan religious structures. Soon most of Egypt's temples were shunned, claimed for other use, or actively destroyed by zealous Christians, and the ancient gods were largely deserted."

Many scholars have noted how the Egyptian beliefs continued even in light of Christianity and Islam trying to destroy it. Osiris' myth along with its central dying and reviving figures, became the cult of Isis that entered Greece when Alexander the Great went to Egypt in 331 BCE and conquered it.

From there, worshipping Isis went to Rome where her cult became the most popular belief within the Roman Empire before Christianity rose and all its opponents after that. Isis Temples have been found all over Egypt from Pompeii to Asia Minor, through all of Europe and into Britain.

The "Dying and Reviving God" that had been established through Osiris was now manifested in Jesus, God's son. With time, epithets for Isis turned into symbols for the Virgin Mary like "Queen of Heaven" and "Mother of God" as Christianity drew on the powers of the older beliefs to get itself established. "The Abydos Triad" of Horus, Isis, and Osiris soon became the Holy Trinity of the Father, the Son, and the Holy Spirit in this new religion that had destroyed all the old beliefs just to reach supremacy.

The Temple of Isis located in Philae in Egypy is thought to be the last pagan temple to have survived all this. In 452 CE, pilgrims visited this temple and got rid of Isis' statue. They carried her to honor her as in the olden days to visit all the neighboring gods in Nubia. When Justinian became emperor in 529 CE, all the pagan beliefs were smothered. There was some resistance to this new religion but the widespread reverence to the old gods was only a memory now.

Wilkinson states: "By 639 AD when Arab armies claimed Egypt they found only Christians and the disappearing legacy of ancient gods who had rules one of the greatest centers of civilization for well over 3000 years."

The goddesses and gods of Egypt wouldn't ever totally vanish. they infused the ideologies of Islam, Christianity, and Judaism. The Five Pillars of Islam that are the profession of faith, pilgrimage, prayer, almsgiving, and fasting were practiced millions of years before by the Egyptians when they worshipped their gods. Heka being an invisible and eternal force that caused creation and sustained all forms of life, was created by the Roman Stoics, Greeks, and the Neo-Platonists as the Nous, and Logos. These philosophies influenced Christianity's development.

In modern times, people call the ancient Egyptian's faith as being a polytheistic, primitive faith but their gods and goddesses were worshipped for over 3000 years. The only conflict that was based on religion was while Akhenaten was reigning between 1353 to 1336 BCE when he insisted on a monotheistic reverence to the god Aten. This was probably a political maneuver to lessen the power of the priests in Amun. For the largest part of Egypt's history, creating a war based on religion would have gone against their most important value that the gods gave to them and this was harmony above all.

Chapter 3: Impact of Mythology on Egyptian

The Pharaohs of Ancient Egypt were god-like. They were also its chief priest or the person that the gods spoke through. Being a descendant of the first king of Egypt, Horus, he would sit on Horus's throne. He would protect his people by making sure Egypt was ruled in ways the gods would approve of with stability, justice, and order.

Priestesses and priests didn't wear anything but white linen so they looked pure and clean for the gods. Male priests would bathe seven times each day and would be shaved totally bald. Some temples would have statues that would be bathed and dressed each day. Almost all the Egyptians would have a name that involved a deity so that it would be hard for them to ignore their religion. The Egyptians were very anxious about their afterlife that they spent their lives trying to please the gods to make sure they would be accepted into paradise. All the Pharaoh's were seen to be Horus's reincarnation. Whatever clan he favored, most of the people would turn to that one. Most pieces of jewelry were based on religion. Art was also full of religious influences. Most everything that was written or drawn was religious. Basically, the goddesses and gods were the Egyptian's life.

Daily Life

Religion was woven into Egyptian's life and pharaoh's power. It would be the deity of a town where the people could ask for help to keep hazards from happening. They would use amulets, folklore, charms, and spells to appeal to the deity to protect them from harm. They would negotiate for anything from the flooding of the Nile, to sowing of the seeds and then harvesting the crops, to protect them from snakes that are poisonous and to have a safe childbirth.

Egyptians spent their lives, building their tombs and were excited to join their families in the afterlife with Osiris. Most family temples and homes that have been found had usahbti figures and idols in a space or niche that was reserved for worship. Even their writing systems of heretic hieroglyphics and cursive included figures of goddesses and gods.

Temples

There are many temples throughout Egypt that show how essential religion was to the ancient Egyptians. It also shows how essential they were to functioning daily. Their religious functions weren't the entire story. Usually one temple would be built very close to another one that whole complexes and cities would rise such as Thebes or Giza. Inside these temples, the Egyptians would perform various rituals which were the main function of their religion. They gave offerings to their gods; they had festivals, and warded off the chaos' forces. These rituals were needed for the goddesses and gods to continue ma'at.

Society, Cosmos, and Kings

The king was the whole of their existence. They guaranteed order. They were the recipient of the benefits that were given by gods including life. They were also the ruler of humanity. He was responsible for the dead, for the dead in general and whoever ruled before him. How he dominated religion would correspond with his political role. During the late predynastic times of about 3100 BCE, the state organizations were based on kingship and their service to the king. The king had superhuman roles as being the manifestation of gods or various other deities that reside on earth.

The king's original title, Horus, proclaimed that he was an aspect of the god Horus, the sky god who can be seen as a falcon. Other identities were added and most notably were the "Son of Ra" and "Perfect God." Both of these were introduced during the Fourth Dynasty, when the pyramids were being built. If a king had the epithet of "Son of Ra" would put the king in a close and dependent relation to the leading figure of the pantheon.

"Perfect God" showed that the king had a status of being a minor deity. To achieve this one had to be "perfected" through his accession into his office. It separated him from the full deities and restricted the extent of his divinity.

While he has an intermediate position between the gods and humans, the king would receive "the most extravagant divine adulation" and would be more prominent than other single gods. When they died, they wanted to have full divinity but he couldn't escape the human context of it. Even though royal funeral monuments were different in type and were a lot bigger. These were also vandalized and pillaged but some of the royal mortuary cults lasted a long time.

There were some kings like Ramses II, some of the Ptolemies, and Amenhotep III tried to get deified during their lives. Others like Amenemhet III became a minor god when they died. These developments demonstrate just how restricted royal divinity truly was. Any king that was divinized would coexist with the mortal self, and many nonroyal people who were kings were deified after they died.

Dead people, humanity, the kings, and gods existed together in the cosmos. The creator god had created out of the chaos all the living beings. All these being would die when the end of time came. The sun god would age and had to be rejuvenated and born again each day. The cosmos was surrounded by and full of disorder that had to be kept away. Disorder was strongest during transition times like the passing from one year into the next or when a king died. Because of this, the king's role in keeping order was universal and not just social. His exact services from his people was needed for the cosmos.

Ma'at or the concept of order was always foremost in the thoughts of Egyptians. The role of the king was to put ma'at anywhere isfet or disorder was found. Ma'at was critical to the Egyptian life and it embraced the notions of moderation, truth, justice, and reciprocity.

Ma'at was personified into a goddess and was considered as the creator's daughter. She received her own cult. For the other deity's cults the king had to offer them ma'at. This encapsulated their relationships between the gods, the king, and humanity. Since the king was humanity's representative, he would return to the gods the order that they sent and the things they were a part of. Ma'at even went into the world of the dead where it is used to weight a soul's heart against it to see if the person can pass into paradise. This shows whether or not the person behaved the right way while they were alive and created order within the world.

Ma'at's role in the lives of humans created a connection between elite morality, political action, and religion.

Over the years, morality and religion were pushed apart due to concerns from the state. This can be seem in the separation between temple and the king. We can't know if morality and religion were as closely integrated for the common people as they were for the elite, or if the elite even believed in these gods. It really doesn't matter because the integration of ma'at, the king, and the universe remains fundamental.

Chapter 4: The Story or Ra
– The Creation Myth

"In the beginning, before there was any land, all was dark, and there was nothing but a great waste of water called Nun. The power of Nun was such that there arose out of the darkness a great shining egg, and this was Ra. Ra was all powerful, and he could take on many forms. His power and the secret of it lay in his hidden name. However, if he spoke other names, that which he named came into being.

'I am Khepra at the down, and Ra at noon, and Atum in the evening,' he said. The sun then rose and moved across the sky and set for the first time.

The he names Shu, and the first winds blew. He named Tefnut the spitter, and the first rain fell. Next he named Geb, and the earth came into being. He named the goddess Nut, and she was the sky arched over the earth with her feet on one horizon and her hands on the other. He named Hapi, and the great River Nile flowed through Egypt and made it fruitful.

After this, Ra name all things that lived upon the earth, and they grew into being. Last of all, he named mankind, and there was man and woman in the land of Egypt. The Ra took on the form of a man and became the first Pharaoh, ruling over the entire country for thousands and thousands of years, and giving such harvest that forever the Egyptians would speak of the good things 'which happened in the time of Ra.'

Since Ra had taken on the form of man, Ra grew old. In time, men no longer feared him or obeyed the laws he had created. They laughed at him, saying, 'Look at Ra. His bones are like silver, his flesh like gold, his hair is the color of lapis lazuli.'

Ra was angered by what he heard the people say, and he was even more angry at the evil deed which men were doing in disobedience to his laws. He called together the gods he had created, Shu, Tefnut, Gebe, and Nut, and he also called upon Nun. Soon the gods gathered around Ra in his Secret Place, and the goddesses as well. But mankind knew nothing of what was going on, and continued to make fun of Ra and to break his laws.

Then Ra spoke to Nun before the assembled gods, 'Eldest of the gods, you who made me, and you gods whom I have made, look upon mankind who came into being at a glance of my eye. See how men plot against me. Hear what they say of me. Tell me what I should do to them. For I will not destroy mankind until I have heard what you advise.'

Nun replied with, 'My son Ra, the god greater than he who made him and mightier than those whom he has created, turn your might eye upon them and send destruction upon them in the form of your daughter, the goddess Sekhmet.'

Ra answered, 'Even now fear is falling upon them and they are fleeing into the desert and hiding themselves in the mountains in terror at the sound of my voice.

'Send against them the glance of your eye in the form of Sekhmet!' cried the other gods and goddesses, bowing before Ra until their foreheads touched the ground.

So with the terrible glance from the Eye of Ra, his daughter came into being. She was the fiercest of all goddesses. Like a lion, she rushed upon her prey, and her chief delight was in slaughter, and her pleasure was in blood. At the request of Ra, she came into Upper and Lower Egypt to slay those who had scorned and disobeyed him. She killed them among the mountains which lie on either side of the Nile, and down beside the river, and in the burning deserts. All whom she saw she slew, rejoicing in slaughter and the taste of blood.

Ra then looked out over the land and saw what Sekhmet had done. He called to her and said, 'Come, my daughter, and tell me how you have obeyed my commands.'

Skehmet answered with her terrible voice of a lioness as she tore into her prey, 'By the life which you have given me, I have indeed done vengeance on mankind, and my heart rejoices.'

Now for many nights the Nile ran red with blood, and Sekhmet's feet were red as she went hither and tither throughout all of the land of Egypt killing and killing. Ra looked out over the earth again, and now his heart was filled with pity for men, even though they had re-belled against him. None of them could stop the cruel goddess Sekhmet, not even Ra himself. She had to stop slaying on her own accord, and Ra saw that this could only come about through his cunning.

He then gave the command, 'Bring before me swift messengers who will run upon the earth as silently as shadows and with the speed of the storm winds.' When these were brought he said to them, 'Go as fast as you can up the Nile to where it flows fiercely over the rocks and among the island of the First Cataract. Go to the isle that is called Elephantine and bring from it a great store of the red ochre which is to be found there.'

The messengers raced off on their way and came back with the blood-red ochre to Heliopolis, the city of Ra, where stone obelisks stood with points of gold that were like fingers pointing to the sun. It was night when they came to the city, but all day the women of Heliopolis had been brewing beer as Ra told them.

Ra walked over to the beer waited in seven thousand jars, and the gods came with him to see how, through his wisdom, he would save mankind.

'Mingle the red ochre of Elephantine with the barley beer,' Ra said, and it was done. The beer now gleamed red in the moonlight, just like the blood of the men.

'Now take it to the place where Sekhmet plans on slaying men when the sunrises,' Ra said. While it was still dark as night, the seven thousand jars of beer was taken and poured out over the fields so that the ground was covered in nine inches, three times the measure of the palms of a man's hand, with the strong beer. This beer has become known as the 'sleep maker.'

When daylight broke, Sekhmet the terrible came through, licking her lips at the thought of the men whom she would slay. She found the place flooded and no living creature in sight. However, she did see the beer, which was the color of blood, and she thought that it was blood, the blood of those whom she had killed.

Then, she laughed with joy, and her laughter was like the roar of a lioness hungry for the kill. Thinking that it was indeed blood, she stooped and drank. She continued to drink, laughing the whole time with delight. The strength of the beer began to build within her brain, so that she could no longer kill. As last she returned back to where Ra was waiting. That day she did not kill a single man.

Ra said, 'You come in peace, sweet one.' Her name was then changed to Hathor, and her nature was changed also to the sweetness of the love and the strength of desire. Henceforth, Hathor laid low men and women only with the great power of love. After this, her priestesses drank in her honor the beer of Heliopolis colored with the red ochre of Elephantine when they celebrated her festival each New Year.

Mankind had been saved, and Ra continue to rule, even though he was old. The time was drawing near when he must leave the earth to reign forever in the heavens, letting the younger gods rule in his place. For dwelling in the form of man, of a Pharaoh of Egypt, Ra was losing his wisdom. He continued to reign, and no one could take his power from him, since that power dwelt in his secret name which none knew but himself. If somebody could discover the his Name of Power, Ra would no longer reign on earth. The only way this could happen would be through the magical arts.

Geb and Nut had children. These were the younger gods whose day had come to rule, and their names were Osiris, Isis, Nephthys, and Seth. Of the children, Isis was the wisest. She was cleverer than a million men, her knowledge was greater than that of a million of the noble dead. She knew all things in heaven and earth, except for the Secret Name of Ra, and that she now set herself to learn by guile.

Ra was growing older with each passing day. As he passed across the land of Egypt, his head shook from side to side with age, his jaw trembled, and he dribbled at the mouth as do the very old men. As his spittle feel upon the ground, it made mud. Isis took this in her hands and kneaded it together as if it had been dough. Then she formed it into the shape of a serpent, making the first cobra, which would forever be the symbol of royalty worn by Pharaoh and his queen.

Isis placed the first cobra in the dust of the road by which Ra passed each day as he went through his two kingdoms of Upper and Lower Egypt. As Ra passed by, the cobra bit him and then vanished into the grass. The venom of its bite coursed through his veins, and for a while, Ra could not speak except for one cry of pain that rang across the earth from the eastern to the western horizon. The gods who followed him crowded round, asking, 'What is it? What ails you?'

But he could not reply and could find no words. His lips trembled and shuddered in all of his limbs as the poison spread throughout his body as the Nile spreads over Egypt at the inundation. At last, he could finally speak. Ra said, 'Help me, you whom I have made. Something has hurt me, and I do not know what it is. I created all things, yet this thing I did not make. It is a pain such as I have never known before, and no other pain is equal to it. Yet who can hurt me? No one knows my Secret Name which is hidden in my heart, giving me all power and guarding me against the magic of both wizard and witch. Nevertheless, as I walked through the world that I have created, through the two lands that are my special care, something stung me. It is like fire, yet is not fire. It is like water, and not water. I burn and I shiver, while all my limbs tremble. So call before me all the gods who have skill in healing and knowledge of magic, and wisdom that reaches to the heavens.'

All of the gods surrounded Ra, weeping and lamenting at the terrible thing which had come upon him. With them came Isis, the healer, the queen of magic, who breathes the breath of life and knows words to revive those who are dying. She said, 'What is it, divine father? Has a snake bitten you. Has a creature of your own creating lifted up its head against you? I will drive it out by the magic that is mine, and make it tremble and fall down before your glory.'

'I went by the usual way through my two lands of Egypt,' Ra responded, 'For I wished to look upon all that I had made. And as I went I was bitten by a snake which I did not see. A snake that I did not create. Now I burn as if with fire and shiver as if my veins were filled with water, and the sweat runs down my face it runs down the faces of men on the hottest days of summer.'

'Tell me your Secret Name,' said Isis, in a sweet and soothing voice. 'Tell me the name, divine father. For only by saying you name in my spell can I cure you.'

Ra then spoke the many names that he had, 'I am the Maker of Heaven and Earth. I am the Builder of the Mountains. I am Source of the Waters throughout all of the world. I am Light and Darkness. I am Creator of the Great River of Egypt. I am the Kindler of the Fire that burns in the sky. Yes, I am Khepera in the morning, Ray at the noontide, and Tum in the evening.'

But Isis did not say a word, and poison made its way through the veins of Ra. She knew that he had only listed the names that all men knew, and that his Secret Name, the Name of Power, was still hidden in his heart.

At last, she said, 'You know well that the name which I need to learn is not among those which you have spoken. Come, tell me the Secret Name. If you do, the poison will come forth and you will have an end to the pain.'

The poison was burning with a great burning, more powerful than any flame of fire. At last, Ra cried out, 'Let the Name of Power pass from my heart and into the heart of Isis. But before it does, swear to me that you will tell it to no other except for son whom you will have, whose name shall be Horus. Bind him first with such an oath that the name will remain with him and be passed on to no other gods or men.'

Isis the great magician swore the oath, and the knowledge of the Name of Power passed from the heart of Ra into hers. Then she said, 'By the name which I know, let the poison go from Ra forever.'

And so the poison passed from him and he had peace, but could no long reign upon earth no longer. Instead, he took his rightful place in the high heavens, traveling each day across the sky in the likeness of the sun itself, and by night crossing the underworld of Amenti in the Boat of Ra, and passing through the 12 divisions of Duat where many dangers lurk.

Ra passes safely, and with him he takes those souls of the dead who know all of the charms and prayers and words that must be said. To make sure that a man doesn't go unprepared for his voyage in the Boat of Ra, the Egyptians painted all of the scenes of that journey on the walls of the tombs of the Pharaohs, with all of the knowledge that was written in *The Book of the Dead*, or which a copy was buried in the grave of lesser men so that they too may read and come safely to the land beyond the west where the dead dwell."

Chapter 5: Isis and Osiris
– Murder and Revenge

"During the days before Ra left the earth, before he had begun to grow old, his great wisdom told him that if the goddess Nut bore children, one of them would end his reign among men. So Ra laid a curse upon Nut so that she should not be able to bear any children.

This made Nut very sad and she decided to go to Thoth for help. Thoth knew the curse of Ra, after it had been spoken, couldn't ever be recalled. But because Thoth was very wise and found a way to escape. Thoth went to the Moon god, Khonsu and challenged him to a contest of checkers. Game after game they played and Thoth always won. The stakes grew even higher, but Khonsu wagered the most, for it was his own light that he might lose.

At last Khonsu couldn't play anymore. Then Thoth gathered up all the light that he ahd won and turned it into five extra days that for ever after were set between the end of the old year and the beginning of the new. A year's length was 360 days before this happened, but the five days that were added, which were not actual days of the year, were held as festival days in ancient Egypt.

After his games with Thoth, Khonsu didn't have enough light to shine the entire month, but dwindled into darkness and then grew to his full glory once again because he had lost light that was needed to make five days.

On the first of these new days Osiris, Nut's oldest son was born. The next day had been set aside as the birthday of Horus the Elder. The third day, Nut gave birth to another son that she called Set, the lord of evil. Nut gave birth to her daughter, Isis on the fourth day. Then on the fifth day, she gave birth to another daughter Nephthys. By doing this, the curse of Ra was both defeated and fulfilled since the days that Nut gave birth didn't belong to any year.

When Osiris was born, many wonders and signs were heard and seen all over the world. The one that was the most notable was a voice that came from the holiest shrine in the temple at Thebes located on the Nile. Today we call that place Karnak. The voice spoke to Pamyles and asked him to proclaim to everyone that Osiris, a mighty and good king, had been born to bring joy to earth. Pamyles did as he was bidden, and he attended to the Divine Child and brought him up as a man among men.

Once Osiris was grown, he married his sister Isis. This was a custom that many Pharaohs in Egypt followed. Set also married Nephthys because a god could only marry a goddess.

When Isis learned Ra's secret name, Osiris became the main ruler of Egypt and reigned on earth just like Ra had done. He found the people to be both brutish and savage. They fought amongst themselves. They killed and ate each other. Isis found both barley and wheat that grew wild on the land with other plants that were not known to man. Osiris taught the humans how to plant the seeds when the Nile rose yearly and sank again leaving fresh fertile land over the fields. He also taught them how to water and tend the crops, how to cut the wheat when it was rips, and how to thresh the grain on the threshing floor, dry it, grind it into flour, and then turn it into bread. He showed them how to plant grape vines and turn the grapes into wine. They already knew how to turn barley into beer.

Once the people of Egypt learned how to make bread and which animal were suitable to eat, Osiris taught them laws and how to live happily and peacefully together. They delighted each other with poetry and music. When Egypt was filled with food and peace, Osiris went all over the world to bring his blessings on other countries. While he was away, he left Isis to rule. She did this both well and wisely.

Since Set was evil, he envied Osiris and hated his sister isis. the more the people of Egypt praised and loves Osiris, the more Set hated him. the more good he did and the happier the people became, the stronger Set's desire to kill Osiris grew because he wanted to rule in his place. Isis was full of wisdom and watched Set to make sure he didn't make any attempts to take over the throne while she was watching the land. Once Osiris came home, Set was among the firs to welcome him home. He even knelt in reverence before Osiris.

But he had already made plans. He was helped by 72 of his evil friends and Aso, the evil queen of Ethiopia. Secretly Set had gotten Osiris's exact measurements and had a beautiful chest made that only Osiris would fit into. It was made from the most expensive and rarest wood... cedar from Lebanon and ebony from Punt located on the south end of the Red Sea because there isn't any wood that grows in Egypt except palms that are useless and soft.

Set had a great feast to honor Osiris but all his other guests were his 72 evil friends. It was the most wonderful feast that ever been seen in Egypt. they had the best foods, the best wine, and the dancing girls were more beautiful than any other girl that had ever seen. Once Osiris's heart was full of food and song, the chest was brought in and everyone was amazed at its beauty.

Osiris marveled at this rare chest with its cedar inlaid with ivory and ebony along with the silver and gold. it had been painted with figures of animals, birds, and gods and he wanted it.

Set announced: 'I will give this chest to whosoever fits in it most exactly!' At once all his evil friends began taking turns to see if they could fit into it. One of them was too tall, another too short, another was too fat, while yet another was too thin. Everyone tried all in vain.

Osiris finally stepped forward: 'Let me see if I will fit into this marvelous piece of art.' he climbed inside and laid himself down in the chest while everyone gathered around.

'I fit exactly,' exclaimed Osiris. 'The chest is mine!'

'It is your indeed, and shall be so forever!' hissed Set as he banged the lid closed. Then in his desperate haste, he and his evil friends nailed the chest shut and sealed all the cracks with molten lead, so that Osiris would die inside the chest and his spirit would go across the Nile to *Duat the Place of Testing*. But he went beyond that into Amenti, where the people who live forever that lived well on earth and passed the judgment of Duat but he could not pass just yet.

Set and his evil friends took the chest that held Osiris's body and threw it into the Nile. Hapi, the god of the Nile carried it out into the Great Green Sea where it was thrown and tossed for several days until it landed on the shores of Pheonicia near Byblos. the waves threw it against a tamarisk tree that grew on its shores. the tree shot out branches and grew flowers and leaves to make a resting place for Osiris's body. It wasn't long before that tree became famous in the land.

It wasn't long before King Malcander heard about it and he along with his wife the Queen Astarte, came to look at the tree. By this time the branches had grown together and hidden the chest that held Osiris's body. The King gave orders that the tree should be cut down and fashioned into a pillar to be placed in his palace. This was done and everyone wondered at is fragrance and beauty. What nobody realized with that it held he body of a god. Back in Egypt, Isis was scared. She knew Set was full of jealousy and evil but Osiris was so kind that he wouldn't believe that Set was evil. Isis knew deep in her heart the moment her husband had died, even though nobody told her. She ran into the marshes carrying her baby with her. She found shelter on a small island there Buto, the goddess lives. She left her baby Horus with Buto to keep him safe from Set. To further safeguard against Set, Isis lossened the island from its foundation and let it float so that nobody would know where to find it.

She then went out to look for the body of her beloved Osiris. Until he was finally buried with all the charms and rites, he spirit couldn't go any further and it certainly couldn't come home to Amenti.

Isis wandered all over Egypt but she could not find a trace of Osiris or the chest. She asked everybody she met, but nobody had seen it and her magical powers could not help her in this matter.

She finally questioned the children who were playing by the river's edge and they told her that a chest just like the one she described ahd floated past them in this swift stream and into the Great Green Sea.

Isis wandered onto the shore and again and it was the children who had seen the chest floating by and told her the way it had gone. Because of their help, Isis blessed the children and decreed that from this time forward, children would be a ble to speak words of wisdom and could tell of things to come.

At length, Isis came to Byblos and sat by the seashore. The maidens who attended to Queen Astarte came to the river to bathe. When they came out of the water, Isis taught them how to plait their hair. They had never done this before. When they went back to the palace a wonderful and strange perfume clung to them. Queen

Astarte loved it and their plaited hair. She asked them how it came to be this way.

The maidens told her of the woman who was sitting on the seashore and Queen Astarte immediately sent for Isis and asked her to serve in the palace and tend to her children, the Prince Maneros and baby Dictys. The baby was very sick. She didn't know that this strange woman was the greatest goddess in all of Egypt. Isis agreed to do this and soon the baby Dictys was very strong and well even though she didn't do anything but give him her finger to suckle. She became very fond of this child and wanted to make him immortal. She did this by burning away all his mortal parts while she flew around him as a swallow. Astarte had been watching her in secret and when she saw what looked like her baby was on fire, she rushed into the room with a loud cry and broke the magic.

Isis then turned back into herself and Astarte crouched down terrified when she saw the shiny goddess and figured out who she truly was.

Malcander and Astarte offered her gifts of all their richest treasures but Isis only asked for the large tamarish pillat the held up their root because of what was inside it. When they gave it to her, she opened it and took out the chest that held her husband's body. The pillar she gave back to the King and Queen. It remained the most sacred object in all of Byblos because it had held the body of a god.

Once the chest which was actually Osiris's coffin had been given to her, Isis flung herself on top of it in a terrible cry of sorrow that caused little Dictys died at the sound of it. Isis finally had the chest placed on a ship that King Malcander had given to her and she set out for Egypt. Maneros went with her but he didn't stay with her for very long because his curiosity proved to be his undoing. As soon as the ship had left the shore, Isis retired to where the chest was at and opened the lid. Maneros crept up behind her and looked over her shoulder. Isis knew he was there and she turned to look at him in anger. he fell backwards over the side of the ship and into the sea.

The next morning, while the ship was passing the Phaedrus River, the strong current almost carried them out of sight of the land. Isis got angry and put a curse on the river so that its water dried up that very day.

She came into Egypt safely from that point. She hid the chest in the marshes while she hurried to the floating island where Buro was guarding Horus.

By chance Set was hunting wild boars with his dogs as hunting at night was his custom because he loved darkness and all things evil were out at night. By the moonlight, he saw the cedar chest and knew immediately what it was.

When he saw it, anger and hatred came upon him in the form of a red cloud. He raged like a panther and tore open the chest. He took the body of Osiris and tore it into 42 pieces and he scattered it all throughout the Nile so that the crocodiles could eat him.

'It is not possible to destroy the body of a god!' Set cried. 'Yet I have done it, for I have destroyed Osiris!' His laughter echoed throughout all the land and anyone who heard it hid and trembled.

Isis had to start her search once again. this time she had others to help her. Her sister, Nephthys had left her evil husband Set and joined Isis on her hunt. Anubis, the son of Set and Nephthys took the form of a jackal helped with the search. Once Isis traveled over the land she was guraded and accompanied by seven scorpions. When she searched on the Nile and in the many streams of the delta, she traveled in a boat that was made from papyrus. the crocodiles, being reverent to the goddess they didn't touch any of Osiris's body parts or Isis. Even after anybody who sailed on the Nile in a boat made from papyrus was safe because they thought it was isis still looking for her husband's body parts.

Piece by piece, Isis found all the fragments of Osiris. When she found a part, she would magically create the likeness of his body and built a shrine in his honor so a priest could perform his funeral. There are 41 places throughout Egypt that claim to be the burial place of Osiris. By doing this, she made it harder for Set to meddle further with his body.

The one piece that she didn't recover was Osiris's penis because it had been eaten by certain impious fishes and their kind became cursed from this point on and no Egyptian would eat or even touch them. Isis didn't bury the pieces where she built a shrine to Osiris. She kept all the pieces together and rejoined them by magic and she magically made a likeness of his penis so that he was complete. She then had the body embalmed and hidden in a place that only she knew where it was. After this, Osiris's spirit went into Amenti to rule the dead until the last great battle, when Horus will slay Set and Osiris will return to earth again.

As Horus grew, Osiris's spirit visited him often and taught him everything that a great warrior needs to know. Anyone who was to fight against Set needed to be strong in spirit and body.

One day, Osiris told his boy: 'Tell me, what is the noblest thing that a man can do?'

Horus answered: 'To avenge his father and mother for the evil done to them.'

This made Osiris happy and he asked: 'And what animal is most useful for the avenger to take with him as he goes out to battle?'

'A horse,' answered Horus.

'Surely a lion would be better still?' suggested Osiris.

'A lion would indeed be the best for a man who needed help,' Horus replied, 'but a horse is best for pursuing a flying foe and cutting him off from escape.'

When he heard this Osiris knew that the time had come for Hours to declare war on Set, and bade him gather together a great army and sail up the Nile to attack him in the deserts of the south.

Horus gathered his forces and prepared to begin the war. And Ra himself, the shining father of the gods, came to his aid in his own divine boat that sails across the heavens and through the dangers of the underworld.

Before they set sail Ra drew Horus aside so he could look into his blue eyes: for anyone who looks into them, of men or gods, sees the future reflected there. But Set was looking and he took upon himself the form of a black pig. He was black as a thunder cloud and fierce to look at. He had tusks that would strike terror into the bravest of hearts.

Ra said to Horus: 'Allow me to gaze into your eyes and see what is to come of this war.' he looked into Horus's eyes and their color was that of the Great Green Sea when the summer sky turns it a deep blue.

While he was looking, the black pig passed by and distracted him, so that he exclaimed: 'Look at that! Never have I seen a pig so fierce and huge.'

Horus looked, and he didn't realize that it was Set, but thought it was a wild boar from the thickets to the north and he wasn't ready with a word or charm of power to guard himself against his enemy.

Then Set aimed fire at Horus's eyes and Horus shouted in pain and was in a great rage. he didn't realize that it was Set but Set had gone away immediately and couldn't be trapped.

Ra had Horus taken to a dark room and it wasn't long before his eyes could see once again just like they did before. Once he had recovered Ra returned to the sky but Horus was full of joy that he could see again and he went up the Nile with his army. The country on both sides shared his joy and bloomed into spring.

There were several battles in that war but the last and greatest was at Edfu, where the great temple of Horus stands even now to memorialize it. The armies of Horus and Set came close to each other among the islands and rapids of the First Cataract of the Nile. Set, in the form of a red hippopotamus that was larger than any normal hippo, sprang up on the island of Elephantine and said a curse against Horus and Isis:

'Let there come a terrible raging tempest and a might flood against my enemies!' he cried, and his voice was like the thunder rolling across the heavens from the south to the north.

At once the storm broke over the boats of Horus and his army; the wind roared and the water was heaped into great waves. But Horus held on his way, his own boat gleaming through the darkness, its prow shining like a ray of the sun.

Opposite Edfu, Set turned and stood at the bay, straddling the entire Nile because he was still in the form of a huge red hippopotamus. But Horus took upon himself the shape of handsome young man that stood 12 feet high. His hand held a harpoon that was 30 feet long with a blade that was six feet wide at its largest width.

Set opened his mighty jaws to destroy Horus and his followers when the storm was about to wreck their boats. Horus cast his harpoon, and it struck deep into the red hippopotamus's head and went into his brain. That one blow killed Set the evil god. All the enemies of Osiris and the other gods along with the huge hippopotamus fell dead beside the Nile at Edfu. The storm quieted, the flood sank, and the sky became clear once again. the people who lived in Edfu came out to welcome Horus, the avenger, and lead him in triumph to the shrine over which the great temple now stands. They sang songs of praise that the priests chanted at each yearly festival for Horus that was held at Edfu:

'Rejoice, you who dwell in Edfu! Horus the great god, the lord of the sky, has slain the enemy of his father! Eat the flesh of the vanquished, drink the blood of the red hippopotamus, but his bones with fire! Let him be cut into pieces, and the scraps given to the cats, and the offal to the reptiles!'

'Glory to Horus of the mighty blow, the brave one, the slayer, the wielder of the Harpoon, the only son of Osiris, Horus of Edfu, Horus the avenger!'

But when Horus passed from earth and reigned no more as the Pharaoh of Egypt, he appeared before the assembly of the gods, and Set came also in the spirit, and contended in words for the rule of the world. But not even Thoth the wise could give judgment. And so it comes about that Horus and Set still contend for the souls of men and for the rule of the world.

There were no more battles of the Nile or in the land of Egypt; and Osiris rested quietly in his grave, which Isis admitted was on the island of Philae because Set could not disturb it. The island of Philae was the most sacred place of all. It was located in the Nile a few miles up from Elephantine. The Egyptians thought that the Last Battles was still to come and that Horus would defeat Set in this one, too. When Set was finally destroyed forever, Osiris would come back from the dead and return to earth. He would bring with him all those who had been his faithful followers. And for this reason, the Egyptians embalmed the dead and set the bodies away beneath towering pyramids of stone and deep in the tomb chambers of western Thebes, so that the blessed souls returning from Amenti should find them ready to enter again, and in them to live forever on earth under the good god Osiris, Isis his queen and their son Horus."

Chapter 6: Horus and Set
– A Mythical Murder Plot Continues

"It was in the 363 year of the reign of the God Ra upon the earth that the great war happened between Horus and Set. Ra was in Nubia with his army, a great and innumerable multitude of soldiers, footmen and horsemen, archers and chariots. He was in his boat made of palm wood, its stern of acacia wood, and he landed at Thest-Hor, to the east of the inner waters. Horus of Edfu approached him. He was looking for the wicked on, Set, who had murdered Osiris. He had long sought out Set, but he had always eluded him.

Ra gathered his forces, for Set had rebelled against him, and Horus was happy with the thoughts of battle. He loved an hour of fighting more than a day of rejoicing. He then found himself in the presence of Thoth, the god of magic. Thoth gave him the power to change himself into a great winged disk. This disk would glow like a ball of fire with great wings on either side like the colors of the sky at sunset when the blue transitions from dark to light, and is shot with gold and flame.

As such, Horus, disguised as a great winged disk, sat on the bow of the Boat of Ra and his splendor flashed across the waters and fell upon his foes as they lay in ambush. Upon his beautiful wings he rose into the air, and against his sneaky enemies, he made a curse. This curse terrible and fear-striking, and stated, 'Your eyes shall be blinded, and you shall not see. Your ears shall be deaf, you shall not hear.'

Immediately, when each of the men looked to the person beside them, they saw a stranger. When they heard their own familiar mother-tongue, it sounded like a foreign language, and they cried out that they were betrayed, and that the enemy had come among them. They turned their weapons on each other, and in the quickness of a moment, many had ceased to live, and the rest had fled. All the while, over them flew the gleaming disk watching for Set. But Set was hidden in the marshes of the North Country, and these men had only been his advance-guard.

Horus flew back to Ra, and Ra embraced him and gave him a drink of wine mixed with water. To this day, men pour a libation of wine and water to Horus at this place in remembrance. Once Horus had drank his wine, he spoke to the Majesty of Ra and said, 'Come and see thine enemies, how they lie overthrown in their blood.'

Ra came, and with him came Astarte, Mistress of Horses, driving her furious steeds. They saw the body-strewn fields where the army of Set had slain each other. This was only the first encounter in the South, and the last great battle had yet to happen.

The associates of Set gathered together and took counsel. They all transformed themselves into crocodiles and hippopotamuses, for these great beasts could live under the water and no human weapon could pierce their hides. They walked up to the river, the water swirling behind them, and rushed the Boat of Ra to overturn it. But Horus and gathered his band of armors and weapon-smiths, and they had prepared arrows and spears of metal, smelted and welded, hammered and shaped, with magical words and spells chanted over them. When the fierce beasts had reached the river in waves of foam, the Followers of Horus drew their bow-strings and let fly their arrows, they cast their javelins, and charged with their spears. The metal pierced the hides and reached the hearts, and of these wicked animals 650 were slain, and the rest fled.

This was the second encounter in the South, and the last great battle still had yet to occur.

The men working for Set fled, some up the river and some down the river. Their hearts were weak and their feet failed for fear of Horus, the Harpooner, the Hero. Those who were facing the South Land fled fastest, for Horus was at their back in the Boat of Ra. With him, came his Followers, their weapons in their hands.

At the south-east of Denderah, the city of Hathor, Horus saw the enemy. He rushed upon them with his Followers, while Ra and Thoth watched the conflict as they waited in the Boat.

Then, the Majesty of Ra said to Thoth, 'See, how he wounds his enemies. See, how Horus of Edfu carries destruction among them.' And after, the men build a shrine in this place in rememberance of the fish, and the gods in the shrine were Ra, Min, and Horus of Edfu.

This was the third encounter in the South, and they had yet to fight the great battle.

They quickly turned the Boat, and swiftly moved downstream, following the fugitives who were running towards the North Land. For a night and a day they followed after the men, and at the north-east of Denderah, Horus saw them. He made haste, he and his followers, and feel upon them, and slew them. The slaughter was great and terrible. This would destroy Set's army in the South in four great encounters, but the last great battle was not yet.

The allies of Set turned towards the lake and towards the marshes of the sea. Horus came behind them in the Boat of Ra, and his form was the form of a great winged disk. With him came his Followers, their weapons in their hands. Then Horus commanded silence, and silence was upon their mouths.

Four days and four nights were spent on the waters, seeking the enemy. But they didn't find any, for their foes had turned their shapes into the shapes of crocodiles and hippopotamuses. They were hidden in the water. The morning of the fifth day, Horus saw them. Immediately, he started to fight, and the air was filled with the noise of the combat, which Ra and Thoth watched the conflict as they waited in the Boat.

The Majesty Ra cried out when he saw Horus like a devouring flame upon the battlefield and said, 'See, how he casts his weapons against them, he kills them, he destroys them with his sword. He then cuts them into pieces, and he utterly defeats them. See and behold Horus of Edfu' At the end of the fight, Horus came back in triumph and he brought 142 prisoners to the Boat of Ra.

This made their first encounter in the North, but it was still not the great battle.

For the enemies, who were upon the Northern Waters, turned their faces towards the canal to reach the sea, and they came to the Western Waters of Mert, where the Ally of Set had his dwelling. Behind them followed Horus, equipped was all his glittering weapons, and he went to the Boat of Ra, and Ra was in the Boat with eight of his train. They were upon the Northern Canal, and backwards and forwards they went, turning and returning, but nothing did they see or hear. Then they went northward for a night and a day they came to the House of Rerhu.

There, Ra spoke with Horus and said, 'Behold, your enemies are gathered together at the Western Waters of Mert, where dwell the Allies of Set.' And Horus of Edfu prayed the Majesty of Ra to come in his Boat against the Allies of Set.

Again, they started to travel further north, where the never-setting Stars wheel round a certain point in the sky, and on the banks of the Western Waters of Mert were the Allies of Set, ready for battle. Horus of Edfu was not delayed a moment, but rushed upon the foe, and with him came his Followers, their weapons in their hands. Death and destruction they dealt to the right and left until the enemy fled before them. When the conflict came to an end, they counted the prisoners. 381 were taken, and these Horus slew before the Boat of Ra, and their weapons he gave to his Followers.

This was the second encounter in the North, but the last great battle had not occurred.

Now, at last, Set himself came forth from his hiding-place. Fierce and savage he is, cunning and cruel. In his nature like a beast of prey, without pity. From where he was hiding, he came forth and roared terribly. The earth and the heavens trembled at the sound of his roaring and at the words which he uttered, for he boasted that he would himself fight against Horus and destroy him as he had destroyed Osiris.

The wind bore the words of his boasting to Ra, and Ra said to Thoth, 'Cause that these high words of the Terrible One be cast down.'

Horus sprang forward and charged at his enemy, and a great fight raged. Horus cast his weapon and killed many, and his Followers fought and prevailed. Out of the dust and the noise of the combat came Horus, dragging a prisoner. The captive's arms were bound behind him, and the staff of Horus was tied across his mouth so that he could not make a sound, and the weapon of Horus was at his throat.

Horus dragged him before Ra, and Ra spoke and said to Horus, 'Do with him as you want.'

Horus fell upon his enemy, and struck the weapon into his head and into his back, and then cut off his head. He dragged the body about by the feet and at last he cut the body into pieces. Thus did he treat the body of his adversary as Set had treated the body of Osiris. This took place on the seventh day of the first month of the season when the earth appears after the inundation. To this day, the lake is called the Lake of Fighting.

This was the third encounter in the North, but the last great battle had still not been fought.

The man Horus had slain had been an Ally of Set, and Set himself was very much alive. He raged against Horus as a panther of the South. He stood up and roared in the face of heaven, and his voice was the voice of thunder. As he roared, he transformed himself into a great snake, and entered into the earth. There were none who had seen him go and none of them had seen him change, but he was fighting against the gods, and by their power and knowledge are they aware of what came to pass. Ra said to Horus, 'Set has transformed himself into a hissing snake and has entered the earth. We must cause that he never comes forth. Never, never no more.'

The allies of Set took courage, knowing that their leader was alive, and they assembled again, and their boats filled the canal. The Boat of Ra went against them, and above the Boat shined the glory of the great winged Disk. Once Horus spotted the enemy gathered together in a single place, he drove at them and routed them and slew them without number.

This had been the fourth encounter in the North, but was still not the last great battle.

Horus remained in the Boat of Ra upon the canal for six days and six night, watching for the enemy, but he saw none. They were all corpses in the water.

Horus sent out his Follower, and they hunted down the enemy, and brought in prisoners. 106 from the East and 106 from the West. They were all slain before Ra in the sanctuaries.

Ra gave Horus and his fighters two cities which are known as the Mesen-cities.

The enemies gathered again in the East and the travelled towards Tharu. They launched the Boat of Ra to follow after them, and Horus transformed himself into the likeness of a lion with the face of a man. His arms were like flint, and his head was the Atef-crown, which is a white diadem of the South Land with feathers and horns, and on either side is a crowned serpent. He rushed after his enemies, and defeated them, and brought 142 prisoners.

Horus proclaimed, 'Let us journey northwards to the Great Green Waters, and smite the foe there as we have smitten him in Egypt.'

Northwards they traveled, and the enemy fled before them, and they soon approached the Great Green Waters, where the waves broke on the shore with the noise of thunder. Thoth arose and he stood in the midst of the Boat, and he chanted strange words over the boats and barges of Horus and his Followers, and the sea fell calm as the sound of the words floated across its waves. There was silence on the Great Green Waters, for the wind was lulled, and nothing was in sight except for the boats of Ra and of Horus.

Ra said, 'Let us sail round the whole extent of the land, let us sail to the South Land.'

They knew that Ra was aware of the enemy. They made haste and sailed to the South Land by night, to the country of Ta-kens, and they came to the town of Shais, but until they reached Shais, they did not see the enemy. Now Shais is on the boarder of Nubia, and in Nubia were the guards of the enemy.

Horus transformed himself into the great winged Disk with gleaming wings outspread, and at either die of him came the goddesses Nekhbet and Uazet, and their form was the form of great hooded snakes with crowns upon their heads. Upon the head of Nekhbet was the white crown of the South Land, and upon the head of Uazet was the red crown of the North Land.

The gods riding in the Boat of Ra cried out and said, 'He has placed himself between the two goddesses. Behold how he overthrows his adversaries and destroys them.'

This is the one encounter in Nubia, but the last great battle had still not been fought.

Then came Ra in his Boat and landed at Thest-Hor, and he gave commandment that in every temple throughout the Two Lands men should carve the Winged Disk, and place Nekhbet and Uazet to the left and the right in their hooded snake crowns.

Some now say that the last great battle is still to come, and that in the end, Horus will kill Set, and that Osiris and all the Gods will reign on earth when their enemy is completely destroyed. But others say that the battle is already ended and that Horus slew the great and wicked Foe who had wrought misery and calamity to all.

This is what they say. After months and years, Horus the child grew into a man. Then came Set with his allies, and he challenged Horus in the presence of Ra, and

Horus came forth, his Followers following after in their boats, with armor and weapons.

Isis created golden ornaments for the bow of the boat of Horus, and she laid them in their places with magic words and spells, saying, 'Gold is at the bow of your boat, Lord of Mesen, Horus, Chieftain of the boat, the great boat of Horus, the boat of rejoice. May the valor of Ra, the strength of Shu, power and fear be around thee. You are victorious, son of Osiris, son of Isis, for you fight for the throne of your father.'

Then Set became the red hippopotamus, great and mighty, and he came from the South Land with his followers, travelling to the North Land to meet Horus. At Elephantine, Set stood up and spoke a great curse against Horus and Isis, and said, 'Let there come a great wind, even a furious north-wind and a raging tempest.' The sound of his voice was like thunder of the East. His words were cried from the southern heaven and rolled back to the northern heaven, a word and a cry from Set, the enemy of Osiris and the gods.

Immediately, a storm broke out over the boats of Horus and his allies. The wind roared, and the watered lashed into great waves, and the boats were tossed around like straw. Horus was able to hold his way. Through the darkness of the storm and the foam of the waves gleamed the golden bow like the rays of the sun.

Horus took the form of a young man. He held a harpoon. Over his head, he brandished the weapon as though it were a reed, and he launched it at the great red hippopotamus which stood in the deep waters, ready to destroy Horus and his allies when the storm should wreck their boats.

Once the first weapon was cast, it struck deep into the head of the great red hippopotamus and entered the brain. Thus died Set, that great and wicked One, the enemy of Osiris and the gods."

Chapter 7: Ma'at
– The Goddess of Mortality

"Ma'at was the daughter of Ra, the sun god and no one could take her principles lightly. If anyone flouted any of these principles, their soul wouldn't make it into paradise.

Ma'at came into existence at the start of creation alongside her father Ra. She was considered to be Ra's first offspring. When she was born is the exact same time that Ra created the universe.

When Ra stepped out of the primordial waters of Nun, Ma'at came with him. If Ma'at hadn't come into being at this time, Ra wouldn't have been able to create the universe. Because of this, she is a very important and old goddess.

It is thought that Heka's powerful magic is what caused Ma'at to come into being. Ma'at was critical to the creation. Without her, Ra's creations wouldn't have ever materialized because her existence allows for truth, balance, and divine order across the entire universe.

Egyptians believe that Ma'at means 'that which is straight.' They thought that without her the seasons, ocean tides, stars, and everything we know about the vast universe would fall into chaos and decay. Ma'at was to the ancient Egyptians what gravity is to us now. Basically, without Ma'at, time and space would collapse without Ma'at's divine order.

Since Ma'at is thought to be the daughter of Hathor and Ra, the sky deities. She is the colossal and divine force that holds all of Ra's creations together. Ma'at was married to Thoth who is the god of wisdom and knowledge. They are always together during the Weighing of the Heart Ceremony.

While Anubis is present, Ma'at's feather gets put on one side of a scale while the dead person's heart is put on the other. This is done in front of a panel of judges that always includes Osiris, the lord of the afterlife. When judgment has been bassed, Thoth will record their verdict.

It is thought that Thoth and Ma'at had eight celestial children that are known as the deities of the Hermopolis. They play a critical role in ancient Egypt.

The most important part of Ma'at was her feather. This was the feather that was uses to weigh a person's heart to see if they were fit to go into the afterlife. She normally wore her feather tucked into her crown.

Ma'at can be seen many ways, she can be standing holding a specter, sitting as a winged goddess, or holding the symbol for ankh or breath of life. Another symbol that is important to Ma'at is her scale. This shows that she keeps everything in the universe balanced. She and the other deities of the underworld use this scale to weight a dead person's heart to see if they can pass on into eternity or if they are cast into nonexistence.

Remember that everybody, no matter their economic or social standing, had to be judged in accordance to her principles. The goddesses and gods could not operate outside her principles.

In order for a deity to be thought of as 'that which is straight,' then they have to realize that Ma'at's significance was beyond comparison. If you compare her to the other goddesses and gods, she didn't have as many temples across Egytp. She didn't need a temple because she was order. This is the reason most people believe she was more of a law than a goddess.

Even though she didn't have many physical monuments, she was revered by every Egyptian. She is very significant since she is the almighty force that flows through the divine bodies of the goddesses and gods. She kept the universe from reverting into a disorderly and primordial state before creation and time.

All the pharaohs looked up to Ma'at. Any pharaoh that was newly crowned would ask for her help to bring morality and balance into their kingdom. She was always the first one anyone called upon if a sacrifice was to be made.

All these rulers were bound to live by Ma'at's principles if they didn't want their household to be cast into complete chaos. Pharaohs knew that contradicting her principles would keep them from entering into paradise.

Once a new pharaoh was crowned, they would present Ma'at to the other gods. This shows the transcendent role that she played within the pantheon.

Akhenaten and Hatshepsut were her most devout followers. The throne that Hatshepsut sat upon was called 'Ma'atkare' or the order is the soul of Ra.

Since she is the deity that gave the world purpose, Ma'at was thought to be omnipresent. She didn't have to have temples or magnificent places of worship. Not having any temples of Ma'at showed that the Egyptians didn't have a need to have a temple for her because the temples of the other gods meant they were worshipping Ma'at, too.

Because her name is synonymous with truth, all Egyptians thought that everyone's soul had to go through the 'Hall of Ma'at.' This is better known as the *Hall of Truths*. This hall was like a court of the underworld where the dead get judged by a panel of judges. this ceremony is commonly known as the 'Judgment of Osiris.' This panel included deities like Osiris, Nephthys, and Isis. Anubis, the jackal god of embalming and funerals is there, too.

Within the Hall of Ma'at, a dead person's heart was weighed against Ma'at's feather. If their heart was heavier that the feather, the sould got eaten by Ammit. Ammit was the devourer of bad souls. This beast had the front legs of a lion, the hind legs of a hippopotamus, and the head of a crocodile.

If the person's heart was lighter than her feather, Anubis would take their soul into the arms of Osiris and on into paradise. Having a light soul meant this person had not been plagued by any sinful thoughts of habits.

The whole proceeding was supported by the *42 Confessions of Ma'at*. It didn't matter what or who the soul was in their previous life, it had to submit itself to the 42 truths."

Chapter 8: Anubis
– A Death Myth

"Anubis was born to the goddess Nephthys. Nephtyhs tricked her brother Osiris into fathering a child with her. Her husband, Set, was furious when he discovered the affair and vowed that he would kill the child as soon as he was born. Nephthys, while tricky and deceitful, did not want her child to die at the hands of Set and did what she had to do to protect Anubis. Once born, she hid him away in the marshes near the Nile River.

Isis, Osiris' wife, discovered the baby hidden away and raised him as her own. Once Anubis had grown into strong adult, he repaid Isis for raising him and became her personal protector.

During the many adventures that Osiris took, he would bring Anubis along with him. On one such adventure, Osiris would die at the hands of his brother Set as revenge for having relations with his wife. Set cut Osiris' body into 14 pieces and scattered them throughout the land. Isis brought together a search party of scorpions, her sister, and Anubis, but they were only able to recovered 13 pieces of Osiris' body. During this search, Isis learned that it was Nephthys who had bore this child with Osiris. Isis used her powerful magic to reconstruct the missing piece.

Once Isis had reconstructed her husband's body, Anubis was asked by the god Ra to embalmed him. This was the first embalmment to ever take place. With some help from Thoth and Horus, he wrapped Osiris' body in cloth and completed the Opening of the Mouth ritual. With this act, Anubis became the patron god of embalmers. When Osiris was buried, Anubis performed the first Egyptian burial rites.

After this, Anubis would become known as the god of death. He was his father's right-hand assistant in the underworld. With his knowledge and expertise of preserving the dead through the mummification process, he was highly revered as their protector.

While Set had managed to kill his brother, he had to make sure that his brother's body was destroyed in order to completely defeat him. After the recovery and embalming of the body, Set plotted to steal it and destroy it once more.

During the embalming of his body, Osiris's body had been kept in the wabet, or place of embalming. Set had watched and knew that Anubis left the wabet each not, so he devised a plan. He would transform himself into Anubis and stroll past the unsuspecting guards and steal Osiris's body. Set wasn't able to make it too far, though. Anubis quickly discovered the theft had taken place and set out in pursuit. Trying to ward off his pursuer, Set transformed himself into a bull. The jackal–god, however, was not intimidated by this. As soon as Anubis captured Set, he castrated him and imprisoned him is Saka, the 17th nome of Egypt.

Not one to be outdone, Set escaped from his prison, and continued on his mission. This time, Set tried to steal Osiris' body in the form of a great cat. The plan did not work, and Anubis caught him once more. The jackal-headed god punished Set by branding him with hot irons. This is why the leopard has spots.

Ever persistent, Set continue to try and steal Osiris's body. This time he transformed himself into Anubis once more, and was, once more, caught. Set was forced to serve as Osiris's throne for all of eternity. That is, until he escaped.

He had many jobs to perform in his godly role. He acted as the Guardian of the Scales, which meant he assisted Ma'at in deciding the fate of the souls. When a mortal passed into the underworld, Anubis guided them to the Hall of the Two Truths, where the fate of the soul would be decided. He would weigh the hearts of the deceased against the weight of a feather. If the heart weighed more than the feather, the female demon, Ammit, would eat the person. However, should their heart weigh less than the feather, Anubis would guide the deceased to Osiris so that they could enter heaven.

Anubis would also oversee the embalming and mummification of the deceased. His daughter, Kebechet, would often help him during the mummification process. The bodies would be covered with herbs and plants because Anubis sniffed the bodies before he mummified them. Anubis also took care of the Opening of the Mouth ceremony, which allowed the deceased to talk and eat once they entered the afterlife.

Since Anubis was an amorphous character, he was also associated with secrets beyond the ken of human beings, as he was knowledgeable in the mysteries of the afterlife. It was for this knowledge that Anubis was seen more as a trusted guide than simply a taker of lives.

Lastly, Anubis was told to watch after the dead. People would carve prayers to Anubis in the tombs. While this would eventually fall under the responsibilities of Osiris, many believe that Anubis still protects the dead.

Anubis understood that death was not an end. Since the dawn of humanity, there has never been a bigger mystery to the mortal experience than that of death. It seems as though the ancient Egyptians, including the great pharaohs, placed a lot of interest in the afterlife into their daily existence. Anubis was the symbol of this great unknown. He was always there to user the dead into the abyss beyond the mind and the body."

Chapter 9: The Book of Thoth

"One Pharaoh of Egypt called Rameses the Great had a son named Setna who was learned in all the ancient writings, and a magician. While the other princes spent their days hunting or leading their father's armies to guard the distant parts of his empire, Setna was happier when left alone to his studies.

Not only could he read the most ancient hieroglyphic writings on the temple walls, but he was a scribe who could write quickly and easily all the many hundreds of signs that go to make up the ancient Egyptian language. Also, he was a magician whom none could surpass for he had learned his art from the most secret of the ancient writings which even the priests of Amen-Ra, Thoth, and Ptah couldn't read.

One day, as he was poured over the ancient books written on both sides of long rolls of papyrus, he came upon the story of another Pharaoh's son several hundred years earlier who had been as great a scribe and as wise a magician as he. Nefrekeptah had read the Book of Thoth by which a man might enchant earth and heaven and know how to talk with the beasts and birds.

When Setna read more and found the Book of Thoth had been buried with Nefrekeptah in his royal tomb located at Memphis, nothing would make him happy until he had found it and learned all these things.

He looked for his brother Anherru and said to him, 'Help me to find the Book of Thoth. For without it life has no longer any meaning for me.'

'I will go with you and stand by your side through all dangers,' answered Anherru.

The two brothers set out for Memphis, and it wasn't hard for them to find Nefrekeptah's tomb. Nefrekeptah was the son of Amen-Hotep who was the first great Pharaoh to have that name. He had reigned 300 years before.

When Setna had made his way into the tomb, to the central chamber where Nefrekeptah was laid to rest, he found the body of the prince lying wrapped in its linen bands, still and awful in death. But beside it on the stone sarcophagus sat two ghostly figures called the Kas. The Kas were figures of a boy and a beautiful young woman. Between them on Nefrekeptah's dead chest lay the Book of Thoth.

Setna bowed in reverence to the Kas and said, 'May Osiris have you in his keeping, dead son of the dead Pharaoh, Nefrekeptah the great scribe; and you also, whoever you be, whose Kas sit here beside him. Know that I am Setna, the priest of Ptah, some of Rameses the greatest Pharaoh of all. I come for the Book of Thoth which was yours in your days on earth. I beg you to let me take it in peace because if not I have to power to take it by force or magic.'

Then said the Ka of the woman, 'Do not take the Book of Thoth, Setna, son of today's Pharaoh. It will bring you trouble even as it brought trouble upon Nefrekeptah who lies here and upon me, Ahura his wife, whose body lies at Koptos on the edge of Eastern Thebes together with that of Merab our son whose Kas you see before you, dwelling with the husband and father whom we loved so dearly. Listen to my tale, and beware!'

Nefrekeptah and I were the children of the Pharaoh Amen-Hotep and, according to the custom, we became husband and wife, and this son Merab was born to us. Nefrekeptah cared above all things for the wisdom of the ancients and for the magic that is to be learned from all that is carved on the temple walls, and within the tombs and pyramids of long dead kings and priests in Saqqara, the city of the dead that is all about us here on the edge of Memphis.

Once day as he was studying what is carved on the walls in one of the most ancient shrines of the gods, he heard a priest laugh mockingly and say: 'All that you read there is but worthless. I could tell you where lies the Book of Thoth, which the god of wisdom wrote with his own hand. When you have read its first page, you will be able to enchant the heaven and the earth, the abyss, the mountains and the sea; and you shall know what the birds, the beasts, and reptiles are saying. And when you have read the second page your eyes will behold all the secrets of the gods themselves, and read all that is hidden in the stars.'

Then Nefrekeptah said to the priest: 'By the life of Pharaoh, tell me what you would have me do for you and I will do it if only you will tell me where the Book of Thoth is.'

The priest answered, 'If you would learn where it les, you must first give me 100 bars of silver for my funeral, and issue orders that when I die my body shall be buried like that of a great king.'

Nefrekeptha did all that the priest asked and when he had received the bars of silver, he said, 'The Book of Thoth lies beneath the middle of the Nile at Koptos, in an iron box. In the iron box is a box of bronze; in the bronze box is a sycamore box; in the sycamore box is an ivory and ebony box; in the ivory and ebony box is a silver box; in the silver box is a golden box; and in that lies the Book of Thoth. All around the iron box are twisted snakes and scorpions, and it is guarded by a serpent that can't be slain.'

Nefrekeptah was beside himself with joy. He hurried home from the shrine and told me all that he had learned. But I feared lest evil should come of it, and said to him, 'Do not go to Koptos to seek this book, for I *know that it will bring great sorrow to you and to those you love.'*

I tried in vain to hold Nefrekeptah back, but he shook me off and went to Pharaoh, our royal father, and told him what he had learned from the priest.

The said Pharaoh, 'What is it that you desire?'

Nefrekeptah answered him saying, 'Bid your servants make ready the Royal Boat, for I would sail south to Koptos with Ahura my wife and our son Merab to seek this book without delay.'

All was done as he wished, and we sailed up the Nile until we came to Koptos. And there the priests and priestesses of Isis came to welcome us and led us to the Temple of Isis and Horus. Nefrekeptah made a great sacrifice of an ox, a goose, and some wine and we feasted with the priests and their wives in a fine house looking out upon the river.

But on the morning of the fifth day, leaving me and Merab to watch from the window of the house, Nefrekeptah went down to the river and made a great enchantment.

First he created a magic cabin that was full of men and tackle. He cast a spell on it, giving life and breath to the men, and he sank the magic cabin into the river. Then he filled the Royal Boat with sand and put out into the middle of the Nile until he came to the place below which the magic cabin lay. And he spoke words of power, and cried, 'Workmen, workmen, work for me even where lies the Book of Thoth!' They toiled without ceasing by day and by night, and on the third day they reached the place where the Book lay.

The Nefrekeptah cast out the sand and they raised the Book on it until it stood upon a shoal above the level of the river.

And behold all about the iron box, below it and above it, snakes and scorpions twined. And the serpent that could not die was twined about the box itself. Nefrekeptah cried to the snakes and scorpions in a loud and terrible cry and at his magical words they became still. None of them could move.

the Nefrekeptah walked unharmed among the snakes and scorpions until he came to where the serpent that could not die lay curled around the box of iron. The serpent reared itself up for battle, since no charm could work on it. Nefrekeptah drew his sword and rushing upon it, smote off its head in a single blow. But at once the head and body sprang back together, and the serpent that could not die was whole again and ready for a fight. Once more Nefrekeptah smote off its head, and this time he cast it far away into the river. But at once the head returned to the body and was joined to the neck, and the serpent that could not die was ready for the next battle.

Nefrekeptah saw that the serpent could not be slain, but must be overcome by cunning. So once more he struck *off its head. But before the head and body could come together he put sand on each part so that when they tried to join they couldn't do so as there was sand between them and the serpent that could not die lay helpless in two pieces.*

Then Nefrekeptah went to where the iron box lay on the shoal in the river; and the snakes and scorpions watched him and the head of the serpent that could not die watched him also; but none of them could harm him.

He opened the iron box and found in it the bronze box. He opened the bronze box and found in it the box made of sycamore wood. He opened the sycamore box and found a box of ivory and ebony. He opened the box of ivory and ebony and found the silver box. He opened the silver box and found the gold box. He opened the gold box and he found the Book of Thoth inside it. He opened the book and read the first page and at once, he had powers over the heavens and the earth, the abyss, the mountains, and the sea. He knew what the beasts and birds were saying. He could hear the fishes talking. He read the next page full of spells and saw the sun shining in the sky, the moon and the stars and knew their secrets. he saw the goods who had always been hidden from mortal sight.

Then, rejoicing that the priest's words had proved true, the Book of Thoth was his, he cast a spell upon the magic men, saying, 'Workmen, workmen, work for me and take me back to the place from which I come!'

They brought him back to Koptos where I sat waiting for him, taking neither food nor drink in my anxiety, but sitting stark and still like one who is gone to their grave.

When Nefrekeptah came to me, he held out the Book of Thoth and I took it in my hands. And when I read the first page I also had power over the heavens and the earth, the abyss, the mountains, and the sea. I also knew what the birds, the beasts, and fishes were saying. When I read the second page I saw the sun, the moon, and the stars with all the gods, and knew their secrets just like he did.

the Nefrekeptah took a clean piece of papyrus and wrote on it all the spells from the Book of Thoth. He took a cup of beer and washed off the words into it and drank it so that the knowledge of the spells entered into his being. But I, who cannot write, do not remember all that is written in the Book of Thoth for the spells which I had read in it were many and hard.

After this we entered into the Royal Boat and set sail for Memphis. But scarcely had be begun to move, when a sudden power seemed to seize our little boy Merab so that he was drawn into the river and sank out of sight. Seizing the Book of Thoth, Nefreheptah read from it the necessary spell, and at once the body of Merab rose to the surface of the river and we lifted it on board. But *not all the magic in the Book, not that of any magician in Egypt could bring Merab back to life. Nonetheless Nefrekeptah was able to make his Ka speak to us and tell us what had caused his death. And the Ka of Merab said, 'Thoth the great god found that his Book had been taken, and he hastened before Amen-Ra, saying 'Nefrekeptah, son of Pharaoh Amen-Hotep, has found my magic box and slain its guards and taken my Book with all the magic that is in it.'*

And Ra replied to him, 'Deal with Nefrekeptah and all that is his as it seems good to you. I send out my power to work sorrow and bring punishment upon him and upon his wife and child.' And that power from Ra, passing through the will of Thoth drew me into the river and drowned me.'

Then we made great lamentation, for our heats were well nigh broken at the death of Merab. We put back to shore at Koptos, and there his body was embalmed and laid in a tomb as befitted him.

When the rites of burial and the lamentations for the dead were ended, Nefrekeptah said to me, 'Let us now sail with all hast down to Memphis to tell our father the Pharaoh what has happened. For his heart will be heavy at the death of Merab. Yet he will rejoice that I have the Book of Thoth.'

So we set sail once more in the Royal Boat. But when it came to the place where Merab had fallen into the water, the power of Ra came upon me also and I walked out of the cabin and fell into the river and was drowned. And when Nefrekeptah by his magic had raised my body out of the river, and my Ka told him all, he turned back to Koptos and had my body embalmed and laid in the tomb beside Merab.

Then he set out once more in bitter sorrow for Memphis. But when it reached that city, and Pharaoh came aboard the Royal Boat, it was to find Nefrekeptah lying dead in the cabin with the Book of Thoth bound upon his chest. So there was mourning throughout the land of Egypt, and Nefrekeptah was buried with all the rites and honors due to the son of Pharaoh in this tomb where he now lies, and where my Ka and the Ka of Merab come to watch over him.

And now I have told you all the woe that has befallen us beause we took and read the Book of Thoth; the book which you ask us to give up. It is not yours, you have no claim to it, and indeed for the sake of it we gave up our lives on earth.

When Setna had listened to all the tale told by the Ka of Ahura, he was filled with awe. But nevertheless the desire to have the Book of Thoth was so strong upon him that he said, 'Give me that which lies upon the dead breast of Nefrekeptah, or I will take it by force.'

Then the Kas of Ahura and Merab drew away as if in fear of Setna the great magician. But the Ka of Nefrekeptah arose from out of his body and stepped towards him saying, 'Setna, if after hearing all the tale which Ahura my wife has told you, yet you will take no warning, then the Book of Thoth must be yours. But first you must win it from me, if your skill is great enough, by playing a game of checkers with me. The first one to 52 points wins. Dare you do this?'

Setna answered, 'I am ready to play.'

So the board was set between them, and the game began. And Nefrekeptah won the first game from Setna, and put his spell upon him so that he sand into the ground to above the ankles. And when he won the second game, Setna sank to his waist in the ground until only his head was visible. But he cried out to his brother who stood outside the tomb: 'Anherru! Make haste! Run to Pharaoh and beg of him the great Amulet of Ptah, for by it only can I be saved, if you set it upon my head before the last game is played and lost!'

So Anherru sped down the steep road from Saqqara to where Pharaoh sat in his palace at Memphis. And when he heard all, he hastened to the Temple of Ptah, took the great Amulet form its place in the sanctuary, and gave it to Anherru, saying, 'Go with all speed, my son, and rescue your brother Setna from this evil contest with the dead.'

Back to the tomb sped Anherru, and down through the passages to the tomb where the Ka of Nefrekeptah still played checkers with Setna. As he entered, Setna made his last nove, and Nefrekeptah reached out his hand with a cry of triumph to make the final move that should win the game and sink Setna out of sight beneath the ground for ever.

But before Nefrekeptah could move the piece, Anherru leapt forward and placed the Amulet of Ptah on Setna's head. And at its touch Setna sprang out of the ground, snatched the Book of Thoth from Nefrekeptah's body and fled with Anherru from the tomb.

As they went they heard the Ka of Anura cry, 'Alas, all power is gone from him who lies in this tomb.'

But the Ka of Nefrekeptah answered, 'Be not sad. I will make Setna bring back the Book of Thoth, and come as a suppliant to my tomb with a forked stick in his hand and a firepan on his head.'

Then Setna and Anherru were outside, and at once the tomb closed behind them and seemed as if it had never been opened.

When Setna stood before his father the great Pharaoh and told him all the had happened, and gave him the Amulet of Ptah, Rameses said, 'My son, I counsel you to take back the Book of Thoth to the tomb of Nefrekeptah like a wise and prudent man. For otherwise be sure the he will bring sorrow and evil upon you, and at the last you will be forced to carry it back as a suppliant with a forked stick in your hand and a fire-pan on your head.'

But Setna would not listen to his father's advice. Instead, he returned to his own dwelling and spent all his time reading the Book of Thoth and studying all the spells contained in it. And often he would carry it into the Temple of Ptah and read from it to those who sought wisdom.

One day as he sat in a shady colonnade of the temple, he saw a maiden more beautiful than any he had ever seen entering the temple with 52 girls in attendance to her. Setna was fascinated with this lovely creature with her golden girdle and headdress of gold and colored jewels, who knelt to make her offerings before the statue of Ptah. Soon he learned that her name was Tabubua, and was the daughter of the high priest of the cat goddess Bastet from the city of Bubastis to the north of Memphis. Bastet was the bride of the god Ptah of Memphis.

As soon as Setna say Tabubua, is seemed as if hathor the goddess of love had cast a spell over him. he forgot all else, even the Book of Thoth and desired only to win her. And it didn't seem as if his suit would be in vain, for when he sent a message to her, she replied that if he wished to seek her, he was free to do so as long as he came secretly to her palace in the desert outside Bubastis.

Setna made his way in haste, and found a pylon tower in a great garden with a high wall around it. There Tabubua welcomed him with sweet words and looks. She led him to her chamber in the pylon and served him wine in a golden cup.

When he spoke to her of his love, she answered, 'Be joyful, my sweet lord, for I am destined to by your bride. But remember that I am no common woman but the child of Bastet the Beautiful and I cannot endure a rival. So before we are wed write me a scroll of divorcement against your present wife; and write also that you give your children to me to be slain and thrown down to the cats of Bastet for I can't endure that they shall live and perhaps plot evil against our children.'

'Be it as you wish!' cried Setna.

He immediately took his quill and wrote that Tabubua might cast his wife out to starve and slay his children to feed the sacred cats of Bastet. And when he had done this, she handed him the cup once more and stood before him in all her loveliness, singing a bridal hymn. Presently terrible cries came floating up to the high window of the pylon. The dying cries of his children, for he recognized each voice as it called to him in agony and then was still.

But Setna drained the golden cup and turned to Tabubua, saying, 'My wife is a beggar and my children lie dead at the pylon foot, I have nothing left in the world but you and I would give all again for you. Come to me, my love!'

The Tabubua came towards him with outstretched arms, more lovely and desirable than Hathor herself. With a cry of ecstasy Setna caught her to min and as he did so, all of a sudden she changed and faded until his arms held a hideous, withered corpse. Setna cried aloud in terror, and as he did so the darkness swirled around him, the pylon seemed to crumble away, and when he regained his senses he found himself lying naked in the deset beside the road that led from Bubastis to Memphis.

the passerby on the road mocked at Setna. But one kinder than the rest threw him an old cloak, and with this about him he came back to Memphis like a beggar.

When he reached his own dwelling place and found his wife and children there alive and well, eh had but one thought and that was to return the Book of Thoth to Nefrekeptah.

'If Tabubua and all her sorceries were but a dream,' he exclaimed. 'They show me in what terrible danger I stand. For if another spell is cast upon me, the next time it will prove to be no dream.'

So, with the Book of Thoth in his hands, he went before Pharaoh his father and told him what had happened. And Rameses the Great said to him, 'Setna, what I warned you of has come to pass. You would have done better to obey my wishes sooner. Nefrekeptah will certainly kill you if you don't take back the Book of Thoth to where you found it. Therefore go to the tomb as a suppliant, carrying a forked stick in your hand and a fire-pan on your head.'

Setna did as Pharaoh advised. When he came to the tomb and spoke the spell, it opened to him as before, and he went down to the tomb and found Mefrekeptah lying in his sarcophagus with the Kas of Ahura and Merab sitting on either side. And the Ka of Ahura said, 'Truly it is Ptah, the great god, who has saved you and made it possible for you to retun here as a suppliant.'

The the Ka of Nefrekeptah rose from the body and laughed. saying, 'I told you that you would retuen as a suppliant, bringing the Book of Thoth. Place it now upon my body where it lay these many years. But do not think that you are yet free from my vengeance. Unless you perform that which I bid you, the dream of Tabubua will be turned into reality.

Then said Setna, bowing low, 'Nefrekeptah, master of magic, tell me what I may do to turn away your just vengeance. If it be such as a man may perform, I will do it for you.'

'I ask only a little thing,' answered the ka of Mefrekeptah. 'You know that while my body lies here for you to see, the bodies of Ahura and Merab rest in their tomb at Koptos. Bring their bodies here to rest with mine until the Day of Awakening when Osiris returns to earth for we love one another and would not be parted.'

Then Setna went in haste to Pharaoh and begged for the use of the Royal Baot. And Pharaoh was pleased to give command that it should sail with Setna where he would. So Setna voyaged up the Nile to Koptos. And there he made a great sacrifice to Isis and Horus, and begged the priests of the temple to tell him where Ahura and Merab lay buried. But, though they searched the ancient writings in the temple, they could find no record.

Setna was in despair. Be he offered a great reward to any who could help him, and presently a very old man came tottering up to the temple and said, 'If you are Setna the great scribe, come with me. For when I was a little child my grandfather's father who was as old as I am now told me that when he was even as I was then his grandfather's father had shown him where Ahura and Merab lay buried. For as a young man in the days of Pharaoh Amen-Hotep the First he had helped to lay them in the tomb.'

Setna followed eagerly where the old man led him, and came to a house on the edge of Koptos.

'You must pull down this house and dig beneath it,' said the old man.

When Setna had bought the house for a large sum from the scribe who lived in it, he bade the soldiers whom Pharaoh had sent with him level the house with the ground and dig beneath where it had stood.

They did as he bade them, and presently came to a tomb buried beneath the sand and cut from the rock. And in it lay the bodies of Ahura and Merab. When he saw them, the old man raised his arms and cried aloud; and as he cried he faded from sight and Setna knew that it was the Ka of Nefrekeptha which had taken on that shape to lead him to the tomb.

So he took up the mummies of Ahura and Merab and conveyed them with all honor, as if they had been the bodies of a queen and prince of Egypt, down the Nile in the Royal Boat to Memphis.

And there Pharaoh himself led the funeral procession to Saqqara, and Setna placed the bodies of Ahura and Merab beside that of Nefrekeptah in the secret tomb where lay the Book of Thoth.

When the funeral procession had left the tomb, Setna spoke a charm and the wall closed behind him leaving no trace of a door. Then at Pharaoh's command, they heaped sand over the low stone shrine where the entrance to the tomb was hidden; and before long a sandstorm turned it into a great mound, and then leveled it out so that never again could anyone find a trace of the tomb where Nefrekeptah lay with Ahura and Merab and the Book of Thoth, waiting for the Day of Awakening when Osiris shall return to rule over the earth."

Chapter 10: The Girl With the Rose-Red Slippers

"During the last days of Ancient Egypt, not many years before the country would be conquered by the Persians, she was rule by a Pharaoh called Amasis. To strengthen his country against the ever present threat of an invasion by Cyrus of Persia, who was conquering all of the known world, he welcomed as many Greeks as wished to trade with or settle in Egypt, and gave them a city called Naucratis to be entirely their own.

In Naucratis, not far from the mouth of the Nile that flowed into the sea at Canopus, there lived a wealthy Greek merchant known as Charaxos. His true home was in the island of Lesbos, and the famous poetess Sappho was his sister. He had spent most of his life trading with Egypt, and in his old age, he settled at Naucratis.

One day, as he was walking in the marketplace, he discovered a great crowed gathered around the place where the slaves were sold. Out of curiosity, he pushed his way into the middle of them, and found that everyone was looking at a beautiful young girl who had just been set up on the stone rostrum to be sold.

It was clear that she was a Greek girl with white skin and cheeks like blushing roses. This sight caught

Charaxos breath, for he had never seen anybody as lovely as she.

Thus, once the bidding started, Charaxos was determined to buy her, and, since he was one of the wealthiest merchants in all Naucratis, he did so without too much trouble.

Once he had bought the girl, he found out that her name was Rhodopis and that she had been carried away by pirates from her home in the north of Greece when she was just a child. They had sold her to a rich man who employed many slaves on the island of Samos, and she had grown up there. One of her fellow slaves was an ugly little man known as Aesop, who had always be rather kind to her and told her the most entrancing stories and fables about birds and animals and human beings.

Once she had grown up, her master wished to make some money out of such a beautiful girl, and had sent her to rich Naucratis to be sold. Charaxos listened to her tale and pitied her. It wasn't long before he became infatuated for her. He gave her a lovely house to live in, with a garden in the middle of it, and servant girls to attend to her. He spoiled her with presents of jewels and beautiful clothes. He gave her things as if she had been one of his own daughters.

One day, a very strange thing occurred as Rhodopis was bathing in the marble-edged pool in her secret garden. The servant girls were holding her clothes and guarding her jeweled girdle and her rose-red slippers, or which she was very proud of, while she soaked in the cool water. It was a summer's day, and even in the north o Egypt, it grew quite hot about noon.

Suddenly, when all seemed peaceful and quiet, an eagle came swooping down out of the clear blue sky. He flew straight down, as if to attack the little group by the pool. The servant girls dropped everything that they were holding and fled, shrieking, to hide among the trees and flowers of the garden. Rhodopis rose out of the water and stood with her back pressed up against the marble fountain at one end of it, gazing with wide, startled eyes.

But the eagle didn't notice any of them. Instead, he had his eyes on something else, and swooped right down and snatched up one of her rose-red slippers in its talons. Then it soared once more up into the air on its great wings and, still holding onto the slipper, flew away to the south over the valley of the Nile.

Rhodopis wept at the loss of her rose-red slipper, feeling sure that she would never get to see it or wear it again. She was sorry, too, for having lost something that Charaxos had given her.

It seemed, as though, the eagle had been sent by the gods, possibly Horus himself since the eagle was his sacred bird. This bird flew straight up the Nile to Memphis and then swooped down towards the palace. During that hour, Pharaoh Amasis sat in the great courtyard doing justice to his people and hearing about the complaints that they wished to bring him. Down through the courtyard the eagle swooped and dropped the rose-red slipper of Rhodopis into the Pharaoh's lap.

The people cried out in amazement when they saw this. Amasis was taken aback as well. He picked up the little rose-red slipper and admired the delicate workmanship and how small it was. He believed that the girl that it belonged to had to be one of the loveliest in the world.

Indeed Amasis, the Pharaoh, was so moved by what had happened that he issued a decree, 'Let my messengers go forth through all the cities of the Delta and, if need be, into Upper Egypt to the very borders of my kingdom. Let them take with them this rose-red slipper which the divine bird of Horus has brought to me, and let them declare that her from whose foot this slipper came shall be the bride of Pharaoh.'

The messengers fell prostrate on the ground and cried, 'Life, health, strength be to the Pharaoh. Pharaoh has spoken and his command shall be obeyed.'

They all set forth from Memphis and went by way of Heliopolis and Tanis and Canopus until they came to Naucratis. This is where they heard about the rich merchant Charaxos and of how he had bought the beautiful Greek girl in the slave market, and how he was lavishing all of his wealth upon her as if she had been a princess put in his care by the gods.

They went to the great house beside the Nile and found Rhodopis in the quiet garden beside the pool.

They presented her with the rose-red slipper, and she cried out in surprise that it was hers. She held out her foot so that they could see how well it fitted her. She begged one of the servant girls to fetch the pair to it which she had kept carefully in memory of her strange adventure with the eagle.

Then the messengers knew that this was the girl whom Pharaoh had sent them to find, and they knelt before her and said, 'The good god Pharaoh Amasis, life, health, strength bet to him, bids you come with all speed to his palace at Memphis. There you shall be treated with all honor and given a high place in his Royal House of Women. For he believes that Horus the son of Isis and Osiris sent that eagle to bring the rose-red slipper and cause him to search for you.'

This type of command could not be disobeyed. Rhodopis bade farewell to Charaxos, who was torn between joy at her good fortune and sorrow at his loss, and set out for Memphis.

When Amasis saw her beauty in person, he was sure that the gods had sent her to him. He did not merely take her into his Royal House of Women, he made her his Queen and the Royal Lady of Egypt. They lived happily together for the remainder of their lives and died a year before the coming of Ambyses the Persian."

Chapter 11: The Princess of Bekhten
– A God Who Saved a Princess

"*During the reign of Rameses III, a large temple was built at Thebes in honor of the Moon-god Khonsu. According to a tradition, which is priests in later time inscribed on a stone stelae, the fame of his Theban representative was so widespread that it reached a remote country called Bekhten.*

A king of Egypt, most likely Rameses III, was in the country of Nehern. This was a portion of Western Syria near the Euphrates, collecting tribute according to an annual custom, when the prince of Bekhten came with the other chiefs to salute his majesty and to bring a gift. The other chiefs brought gold, and lapis lazuli, and turquoise, and precious woods, but the prince of Bekhten brought with his offerings his eldest daughter, who was very beautiful. The king accepted the maiden, and took her to Egypt, where he made her the chief royal wife and gave her the name of Ra-neferu, meaning the beauties of Ra.

Some time later, in the 15th year of the reign of the king of Egypt, the prince of Bekhten appeared in Thebes on the 22nd day of the second month of summer. Once he was taken into the presence of the king, he laid his offering at the feet of the king, and did honor him. As soon as he had the chance, he explained the object of his visit to Egypt, and said that he had come on behalf of the young sister of Queen Ra-neferu, who was seriously ill, and he begged the king to send a physician to see his daughter Bent-Reshet.

The king then called in all of the learned men of his court, and asked them to choose from among their many skilled physicians that he might go to Bekhten and heal the Queen's young sister. The royal scribe Tehuti-em-beb was recommended for this purpose, and the king at once sent him off with the envoy from Bekjten to that country.

It was long after their arrival that they found that the princess of Bekhten was under the influence of some type of evil spirit. This spirit was powerless either to exercise to contend with in any way that would prove to be successful. When the king of Bekhten saw that his daughter was in no way benefited by the Egyptian scribe, he dispatched his delegate a second time to Egypt with the petition that the king would send a god to heal his daughter, and the delegate arrived in Thebes at the time when the king was celebrating the festival of Amon.

As soon as the king got word of what was wanted, he went to the temple of Khonsu Neffer-hetep, and said to the god, 'My fair Lord, I have come once again into the your presence to ask of you on behalf of the daughter of the Prince of Bekhten,' and he asked him to allow the god Khonsu to go to Bekhten, as said, 'Grant that you magical power may go with him, and let me send his divine Majesty into Bekhten to deliver the daughter of the Prince of that land from the power of the demon.'

The king of Egypt sent Khonsu to Bekhten, where the god arrived after a 17 month journey. As soon as he was welcomed into the country by the Prince of Bekhten and his generals and nobles, the god went to the place where the princess was, and he found that Bent-reshet was possessed of an even spirit. As soon as the god use his magical power on the demon, it left the women and she was quickly healed. Then the demon spoke to Khonsu. The demon acknowledged his power, and having tendered to him his unqualified submission, he offered to return to his own place. He begged Khonsu to ask the Prince of Bekhten to make a feast at which they could both be present, and he did so, and the god, demon, and the Prince spent a very happy day together. When the feast was over, the demon returned to his own land, which he loved, according to his promise.

Once the Prince had realized the power of Khonsu, he planned on keeping him in Bekhten, and the god actually lived there for three years, four months, and five days, but in time, he left from his shrine and returned to Egypt in the form of a hawk of gold.

Once the king saw what had happened, he spoke to the priest, and declared to him his determination to send back to Egypt the chariot of Khonsu, and when he had loaded him with gifts and offerings of every kind the

Egyptians set out from Bekhten and made the journey back to Thebes in safety.

Once he returned, Khonsu took all of the gifts which had been given to him by the Prince of Bekhten, and carried them to the temple of Khonsu Nefer-hetep, where he laid them at the feet of the go. And that is the story which the priests of Khonsu, under the New Empire, were won't t relate concerning their god 'who could perform mighty' deeds and miracles, and vanquish the demons of darkness."

Chapter 12: The Seven Year Famine

The following story comes to us from the famous inscription that was found on a rock on the Island of Sahal. It was discovered in 1890 by Charles Wilbour.

"During the 18th year of King Tcheser, who was the third king of the third dynasty, the entire region of the South, the district of Nubia, and the Island of Elephantine were ruled by the high official Mater. The King sent a message to Mater, letting him know that he was in a lot of grief due to the reports that were brought to him into the palace as he was sitting on his throne. He was also upset by the fact that for seven years, there had been no satisfactory flood of the Nile. Due to this, the grain of every kind was very scarce, vegetables and garden produce of all kinds couldn't be found, and most people didn't have much to eat. The people were in such need, they had resorted to robbing their neighbors. Men wanted to walk out, but they couldn't do it because they didn't have the strength. Children cried for food, and young men were collapsing due to the lack of food. The spirits of the aged were crushed to the earth, and they laid themselves down on the ground to die.

Within all of this terrible trouble, King Techeser remembered the god Imhotep, the son of Ptah of the
South Wall, who, it would seem, had once helped
Egypt out in a similar situation. This help was no longer
there, Tcheser asked his governor Mater to tell him
where the Nile rose, and what deity was in charge of it.

In response to his letter, Mater made his way, immediately, to the King and gave him the information that he
wanted on the matters he had asked about. He told him
that the Nile flood started in Elephantine where the first
city ever existed. Out of that space rose the sun when
he started to give life to man, and therefore, it is known
as , 'Doubly Sweet Life.' The area of the island where
the river rose was the double cavern Qerti, which appeared as two breasts, from which all good things
poured forth. This double cavern was the 'couch of the

Nile,' and from it the Nile-god watched until the season of flooding drew closer, and then he rushed forth like a young man and filled the whole country. At Elephantine he grew to a height of 46 feet, but Diopolis Parva in the Delta he only rose 10 ½ feet. The guardian of this flood was Khnemu, and it was he who kept the doors that held in the flood, and who drew back the bolts at the right time.

Mater continued on and described the temple of Khnemu at Elephantine and told his royal master that the other gods there were Sopdet, Nephthys, Isis, Horus, Osiris, Nut, Geb, Shy, Hapi, and Anqet. After this, he listed the different products that were found in the neighborhood, and from which offerings should be given to Khnemu. When the King heard all of this, he offered up sacrifices to the god, and soon enough, he traveled to his temple to make supplication before him.

Lastly Khnemu came before him, and said, 'I am Khnemu the Creator. My hands rest upon thee to protect they person, and to make sound they body. I gave thee thine heart. I am he who created himself. I am the primeval watery abyss, and I am the Nile who riseth at his will to give health for me to those who toil. I am the guide and director of all men, the Almighty, the father of the god, Shu, the mighty possessor of earth.'

Eventually, the god made a promise that the Nile should rise every year, as it use to, and described the good which should come upon the land when he had made an end of the famine. When Khnemu ceased to speak, King Tcheser remembered that the god had complained the nobody took the trouble to fix his shrine, even thought stone laide nearby in abundance, and he immediately issued a decree in which it was ordered that certain land s on each side of the Nile near Elephantine should be set apart for the endowment of the temple of Khnemu, and that a certain tax should be levied upon every product of the neighborhood, and devoted to the maintenance of the priesthood of the god. The original text of the decree was written upon wood, and as this was not lasting, the King ordered that a copy of it be cut in a stone stele, which should be placed in a prominent area."

It is not known if Khnemu kept the promise he made to Tscher, but we could assume that he did. The form of this story as told above is no older than the Ptolemaic period, but the subject of the story belongs to a much older time, and likely represents a tradition that dates back to the Early Empire.

Chapter 13: The Golden Lotus

"Seneferu, father of the Pharaoh Khufu who built the Great Pyramid of Giza, reigned long over a contented and peaceful Egypt. He had no foreign wars and few troubles at home, and with so little business of state he often found time hanging heavy on his hands.

One day he wandered wearily through his palace at Memphis, seeking for pleasures and finding none that would lighten his heart.

Then he asked that his Chief Magician, Zazamankh come to him, and he said, 'If any man is able to entertain me and show me new marvels, surely it is the wise scribe of the rolls. Bring Zazamankh before me.'

Straightway his servants went to the House of Wisdom and brought Zazamankh to the presence of Pharaoh. And Seneferu said to him, 'I have sought throughout all my palace for some delight and found none. Now of your wisdom devise something that will fill my heart with pleasure.'

Then said Zazamankh to him, 'Oh, Pharaoh life, health, strength be to you! My counsel is that you go sailing upon the Nile, and upon the lake below Memphis. This will be no common voyage, if you will follow my advice in all things.'

'Believing that you will show me marvels, I will order out the Royal Boat,' said Seneferu. 'Yet I am weary of sailing upon the Nile and upon the lake.'

'This will be no common voyage,' Zazamankh assured him. 'For your rowers will be different from any you have seen at the oars before. They must be fair maidens from the Royal House of the King's Women: and as you watch them rowing, and see the birds upon the lake, the sweet fields and the green grass upon the banks, your heart will grow glad.'

'Indeed, this will be something new,' agreed Pharaoh, showing some interest at last. 'Therefore I give you charge of this expedition. Speak with my power, and command all that is necessary.'

Then said Zazamankh to the officers and attendants of Pharoah Seneferu, 'Bring me twenty oars of ebony in-laid with gold, with blades of light wood inlaid with electrum and bring 20 of the fairest maidens to be the rowers. The 20 virgins need to be lovely and slim, fair in their limbs, beautiful, and with flowing hair and bring me 20 nets of golden thread, and give these nets to the fair maidens for their garments. Let them wear orna-ment made from malachite, electrum, and gold.'

All was done according to the words of Zazamankh, and presently Pharaoh was seated in the Royal Boat while the maidens rowed him up and down the stream and upon the shining waters of the lake. And the heart of Seneferu was glad at the sight of the beautiful rowers at their unaccustomed task, and he seemed to be on a voyage in the golden days that were to be when Osiris returns to rule the earth.

But presently a mischance befell that gay and happy party upon the lake. In the raised stern of the Royal Boat two of the maidens were steering with great oars fastened to posts. Suddenly the handle of one of the oars brushed against the head of the girl who was using it and swept the golden lotus that she wore on the head-band that held her hair back into the water and it sank out of sight.

With a cry, she leant over the side of the boat and gazed after it. Since she has stopped singing to look for her lotus, all the other rowers stopped singing, too.

'Why have you stopped rowing?' asked Pharaoh.

They replied, 'Our little rower has stopped, and leads us no longer.'

'And why have you ceased to steer and lead the rowers with your song?' asked Seneferu.

'Forgive me, Pharaoh, life, health, strength be to you!' she sobbed. 'But the oar struck my hair and brushed from it the beautiful golden lotus set with malachite which your majesty gave to me, and it has fallen into the water and is lost forever.'

'Row on as before, and I will give you another,' said Seneferu.

But the girl continued to weep, saying, 'I want my golded lotus back, and no other!'

Then said Pharaoh, 'There is only one who can find the golden lotus that has sunk to the bottom of the lake. Bring to me Zazamankh my magician, he who thought of this voyage. Bring him here on to the Royal Boat before me.'

So Zazamankh was brought to where Seneferu sat in his silken pavilion on the Royal Boat. And as he knelt, Pharaoh said to him: 'Zazamankh, my friend and brother, I have done as you advised. My royal heart is refreshed and my eyes are delighted at the sight of these lovely rowers bending to their task. As we pass up and down on the waters of the lake, and they sing to me, while on the shore I see the trees and the flowers and the birds. I seem to be sailing into the golden days either when Ra ruled the earth, or those to come when the god Osiris shall return from the Duat. But now a golden lotus has fallen from the hair of one of these maidens and fallen to the bottom of the lake. And she has ceased to sing and the rowers on her side cannot keep time with their oars. And she is not to be comforted with promises of other gifts, but weeps for her golden lotus. Zazamankh, I wish to give back the golden lotus to the little one here, and see the joy return to her eyes.'

'Pharaoh, my lord life, health, strength be to you!' answered Zazamankh the magician, 'I will do what you ask, for to one with my knowledge it is not a great things. Yet maybe it is an enchangement you have never seen, and it will fill you with wonder, even as I promised, and make your heart rejoice yet further in new things.'

Then Zazamankh stood at the stern of the Royal Boat and began to chant great spells and words of power. And presently he held out his wand over the water, and the lake parted as if a piece had been cut out of it with a great sword. The lake here was 20 feet deep, and the piece of water that the magician moved rose up and set itself upon the surface of the lake so that there was a cluff of water on that side 40 feet high.

Now the Royal Boat slid gently down into the great cleft in the lake until it rested on the bottom. On the side towards the 40-foot cliff of water, there was a great open space where the bottom of the lake lay uncovered, as firm and dry as the land itself.

And there, just below the stern of the Royal Boat, lay the golden lotus.

With a cry of joy, the maiden who had lost it sprang over the side on to the firm ground, picked it up and set it once more in her hair. Then she climbed swiftly back into the Royal Boat and took the steering oar into her hands once more.

Zazamankh slowly lowered his rod, and the Royal Boat slid up the side of the water until it was level with the surface once more. Then at another word of power, and as if drawn by the magician's rod, the great piece of water slid back into place, and the evening breeze rippled the still surface of the lake as if nothing out of he ordinary had happened. But the heart of Pharaoh Seneferu rejoiced and was filled with wonder he cried: 'Zazamankh, my brother, you are the greatest and wisest of magicians! You have shown me wonders and delights this day, and your reward shall be all that you desire and the place next to my own in Egypt.'

Then the Royal Boat sailed gently on over the lake in the glow of the evening, while the 20 lovely maidens in their garments of golden net, and the jeweled lotus flowers in their hair dipped their ebony and silver oars in the shimmering waters and sang sweetly a long song of old Egypt:

She stands upon the further side,

Between us flows the Nile;

And in those water deep and wide

There lurks a crocodile.

Yet is my love so true and sweet,

A word of power, a charm

The stream is land beneath my feet

And bears me without harm.

For I shall come to where she stands,

No more be held apart;

And I shall take my darling's hands

And draw her to my heart."

Chapter 14: The Prince
and The Sphinx

"There once was a Prince of Egypt called Thutmose, who was a son of Pharaoh Amenhotep, and the grandson of Thutmose III who succeeded the great Queen Hatsepsut. He had many brothers and half-brothers, and because he was Pharaoh's favorite son they were forever plotting against him. Usually these plots were to make Pharaoh think that Thutmose was unworthy or unsuitable to succeed him; sometimes they were attempts to make the people or the priests believe that Thutmose was cruel or extravagant or did not honor the gods and so would make a bad ruler of Egypt; but once or twice the plots were aimed at his very life.

All this made Thutmose troubled and unhappy. He spent less and less of his time at Thebes or Memphis with Pharaoh's court, and more and more frequently rode on expeditions into Upper Egypt or across the desert to the seven great oases. And even when Pharaoh commanded his presence, or his position demanded that he must attend some great festival, he would slip away whenever he could with a few trusted followers, or even alone and in disguise, to hunt on the edge of the desert.

Thutmose was skilled in all manly exercises. He was a bowman who could platn arrow after arrow in the center of the target; he was a skilled charioteer, and his horses were faster than the wind. Sometimes he would course antelopes for miles across the sandy stretches of desert; at other he would seek out the savage lions in their lairs among the rocks far up above the banks of the Nile.

One day, when the court was in residence at Memphis for the great festival of Ra at Heliopolis a few miles further down the Nile, Thutmose excaped from all the pomp and pageantry to hunt on the edge of the desert. He took with him only two servants, and he drove his own chariot up the steep road past Saqqara where the great Step Pyramid of Djoser stands, and away through the scrub and stunted trees where the cultivated land by the Nile faded into the stony waste and the stretches of sand and rock of the great Libyan desert.

They set off at the first glimmer of dawn so that they might have as much time as possible before the great heat of midday, and they coursed the gazelle northwards over the desert for many miles, parallel to the Nile but some miles away from it.

By the time the sun grew too hot for hunting, Thutmose and his two followers had reached a point not very far away from the great Pyraminds of Giza which the Pharaohs of the Fourth Dynasty had built over 1200 years before.

They stopped to rest under some palm trees. But presently Thutmose, desiring to be alone and wishing to make his prayer to the great god Harmachis, entered his chariot and drove away over the desert, bidding his servants wait for him.

Away sped Thutmose, for the sand was firm and smooth, and at last he drew near to the three pyramids of Khufu, Khafra, and Mendaura towering up towards the sky, the burning sun of midday flashing on their golden peaks and glittering down their polished sides like ladders of light leading up to the Boat of Ra as it sailed across the sky.

Thutmose gazed in awe at these manmade mountains of stone. But most of all his attention was caught by a gigantic head and neck of stone that rose out of the sand between the greatest of the pyramids and a nearly buried mortuary temple of huge squared stone blocks that stood on either side of the stone causeway leading from the distant Nile behind him right to the foot of the second pyramid; that of the Pharaoh Khafra.

This was a colossal carving of Harmachis the god of the rising sun, in the form of a lion with the head of a Pharaoh of Egypt. The form he had taken when he became the hunter of the followers of Set. Khafra had caused this 'sphinx' to be carved out of an outcrop of solid rock that happened to rise above the sand near the processional causeway leading from the Nile to his great pyramid. And he had bidden his sculptors shape the head and face of Harmachis in the likeness of his own.

During the long centuries since Khafra had been laid to rest in his pyramid the sands of the desert had blown against the Sphinx until it was almost buried. thutmose could see no more than its head and shoulders, and a little ridge in the desert to mark the line of its back. For a long while he stood looking up into the majestic face of the Sphinx, crowned with the royal crown of Egypt that had the cobra's head on its brow and which held in place the folds of embroidered linen which kept the sun from head and neck; only here the folds were of stone and only the head of the serpent fitted onto the carved rock was of gold.

The noonday sun beat mercilessly down upon Thutmose as he gazed up at the Sphinx and prayed to Harmachis for help with all his troubles.

Suddenly it seemed to him that the great stone image began to stir. It heaved and struggled as if trying in vain to throw off the sand which buried its body and paws, and the eyes were no longer carved stone inlaid with lapis lazuli, but shone with life and vision as they looked down upon him. Then the Sphinx spoke to him in a great voice, and yet kindly as a father would speak to his son.

'Look upon me, Thutmose, Prince of Egypt, and know that I am Harmachis your father; the father of all Pharaohs of the Upper and Lower Lands. It rests with you to become Pharaoh indeed and wear upon your head the Double Crown of South and North; it rests with you whether or not you sit-upon the throne of Egypt, and whether the peoples of the world come and kneel before you in homage. If you indeed become Pharaoh whatever is produced by the Two Lands shall be yours, together with the tribute from all the countries of the world. Besides all this, long years of life, health and strength shall be yours.'

'Thutmose, my face is turned towards you, my heart inclines to you to bring you good things; your spirit shall be wrapped in mine. But see how the sand has closed in round me on every side; it smothers me, it holds me down, it hides me from your eyes. Promise me that you will do all that a good son should do for his father; prove to me that you are indeed my son and will help me. Draw near to me, and I will be with you always, I will guide you and make you great.'

Then as Thutmose stepped forward the sun seemed to shine from the eyes of Harmachis the Sphinx so brightly that they dazzled him and the world went black and spun around him so that he fell insensible on the sand.

When he recovered, the sun was sinking towards the summit of Khagras' pyramid and the shadow of the Sphinx lay over him.

Slowly he rose to his feet, and the vision he had seen came rushing back into his mind as he gazed at the great shape half-hidden in the sand which was already turning pink and purple in the evening light.

'Harmachis, my father!' he cried, 'I call upon you and all the gods of Egypt to bear witness to my oath. If I become Pharaoh, the first act of my reign shall be free this your image from the sand and build a shrine to you and set in it a stone telling in the sacred writing of Khem of your command and how I fulfilled it.'

Then Thutmose turned to seek his chariot; and a moment later his servants, who had been anxiously searching for him, came riding up.

Thutmose rode back to Memphis, and from that day all went well with him. Very soon Amenhotep the Pharaoh proclaimed him publicly as heir to the throne; and not very long afterwards Thutmose did indeed become King of Egypt one of her greatest Kings."

Chapter 15: The Greek Princess

"During the time when Seti II, who was the grandson of Rameses the Great, was the Pharaoh of Egypt, there came a great ship driven by a storm from the north that sought shelter in the Canopic mouth of the Nile.

Near the place where the ship anchored stood the temple of the ram-headed god Hershef, who watched over strangers. If any man took sanctuary in the shrine of Hershef, he would be safe from all his enemies; and if a slave knelt before the statue and vowed to serve the god, he became free from his master.

the ship which had come to Canopus was reported at once to Thonis, the Warden of the mouth of the Nile, and he learned that it belonged to a prince of the people whom the Egyptians call the People of the Sea, or the Aquaiusha that is the Achaeans, those who dwelt in Greece and the islands of the Aegean and in Ionia, whom we now call the Mycenaeans.

Thonis discovered this from a group of the sailors on the ship who, when they learned of what chanced to those who sought sanctuary in the Temple of Hershef, deserted in a body and asked to be allowed to serve the god. When Thonis asked them why they wished to leave their master, since it seemed strange to him that men of the Aquaiusha, should wish to enter the service of an Egyptian god rather than return to their homes, they replied that they feared the vengeance of their own gods if they remained on the ship.

For it seemed that the Prince their master had carried off the wife of one of the kings of Greece, together with much of his treasure, and this after the Greek king had received him as a guest and friend, and entertained him kindly in his palace.

Thonis was as much shocked as the sailors by this behavior, for in Egypt as in Greece to behave thus to one's host was thought to bring a sure vengeance from the gods. And he seized the Prince's ship with all on it and guraded it closely until he learned the will of Pharaoh. But the Greek Princess he caused to be escorted with all honor to the Temple of Hathor, the goddess of love and beauty.

When Seti heard of all this, he commanded Thonis to bring the ship, with all who had sialed in her, up the Nile to Memphis.

All was done as he commanded, and when they arrived the Princess was placed for safety in the Temple of Hathor at Memphis. But the Prince was led at once before Seti where he sat in his great hall of audience.

'Oh, Pharaoh, life, health, strength be to you!' cried Thonis, kissing the ground before Seti's feet according to custom. 'I bring before you this stranger, a prince of the Aquaiusha, that you may learn from his own mouth who he is and why he has come to your shores.'

The Seti spoke kindly to the stranger Prince, saying, 'Welcome to the land of Egypt, if you come in peace and as one who serves the gods. My Warden of the Nile, Thonis, tells me that in your own land you are the son of a king. Tell me of that land of that king, for it is my delight to hear strange stories and tales of other lands.'

The handsome young Prince in his bronze armor that shone like gold bowed before Pharaoh and said, 'My lord, I come in peace, driven here against my will by the god of the sea whom we call Poseidon. I am the som of Priam, the great King of Troy, and I have been on a visit to Greece where I have won to be my wife the most beautiful woman in the world, Helen, Princess of Sparta, and daughter of its King, Tyndareus.'

Seti the Pharaoh looked thoughtfully at the proud young Prince, and said, 'Tell me, Prince of Troy, how did you come to win this Princess of Sparta? Do the kings of the Aquaiusha send their daughters across the sea to be wedded to the princes of other lands? For my learned scribe Ana, here, tells me that the city of Troy is far across the water from the land and islands of the Aquaiusha, and that there is war and rivalry between the two lands.'

'Then your scribe Ana is in error,' answered the Prince loftily. 'There was some fighting in my grandfather's day, but since then we have dwelt at peace. I came as one of the many princes of the Aquaiusha who were suitors for the hand of fair Helen, and King Tyndareus of Sparta gave her to me.'

At this the sailors who had sought sanctuary in the Temple of Hershef murmured, and Seti the Pharaoh said to them, 'Thonis reports that you who are now servants of Hershef tell another tale concerning these matters. Speak without fear, for you are now my subjects, and I will protect you.'

'King of Egypt,' answered the leader, 'we few sailors come from the islands and are of the Greek people, whom you call Aquaiusha, not men of Troy, whom we hold to be barbarians. We serve the gods of Greece and we fear them also and know that they punish wrongdoing.'

'This man, Prince Paris of Troy, who was our master, came as he says as a friend to Sparta but he does not speak the truth of what happened there. All the people of our lands have heard of Helen, the most beautiful woman in the world, the daughter of King Tyndareus of Sparta and Ledz his Queen, though it is said that in truth Zeus, King of the Gods, whom you call Amon-Ra, was her father.'

Seti nodded when he heard this and murmured, 'Even as Amon-Ra was the father of Hatshepsut, the Great Queen of Egypt. Yes, the gods can indeed be the fathers of the spirits that dwell in the bodies of kings and queens.'

'The princes of Greece and of the islands all sought the land of Helen in marriage,' went on the sailor, 'not only for her beauty but also because whoever married her would become the King of Sparta. But Paris of Troy was not among their number. No, King Tyndareus gave his daughter to Menelaus, the younger son of the King of Mycenae, and made all the rest of her suitors swear to abide by his choice and to stand by Menelaus should anyone strive to steal his wife. That was several years ago. Since then Tyndareus has made Menelaus King of Sparta and he has reigned there with Helen as his Queen. The Prince of Troy came as a guest and an ambassador, and was welcomed as such. He dwelt at Sparta for many days, until Menelaus was forced to leave the city for a while on some affair of state. When he was gone, Paris carried off Helen by force, together which much treasure, and sailed away only to be caught in a storm sent by the angry gods and driven hither.'

'That is false!' shouted Prince Paris angrily. 'Helen came of her own free will. She begged me to take her, for she hated her husband, Menelaus! And the treasure we took with us was her own.'

'Prince of Troy,' said Seti the Pharaoh, 'You have already told me two tales which do not agree. First you say that you won this princess from her father when all the princes of the Aquaiusha came as her suitors, and then you admit that you took her from the husband whom her father had chosen for her and made King of Sparta… Vizier, lead this prince of Troy with all honor to the royal Guest-House and see that he and his followers are well guarded and ready to appear before me again when I command their presence.'

'Pharaoh has spoken life, health, strength be to him!' cried Para-em-heb the Vizier, prostrating himself before Seti. Then at a sign from him the guards closed in and led the Prince of Troy and his followers away.

'And now,' said Seti the Pharaoh, 'we will visit this princess of the Aquaiusha where she dwells in the Temple of Hathor.'

Seti and his companions, the scribe Ana and Roi the High Priest of Amon-Ra, made their way to the Temple of Hathor where the lovely Princess Helen had been lodged in the care of the priestesses of the goddess.

When he beheld her, Seti felt that he was indeed in the presence of the loveliest woman in the world, perhaps even a goddess upon earth.

The tale of the Princess was far different from that of the Prince. According to her, she had dwelt in great happiness with her husband Menelaus and her two children, and felt no love at all for Paris the Trojan. Indeed, from what she told him, Seti understood that Paris had carried her off by magic, taking upon himself the shape of Menelaus to lure her away from the palace, down the long valley to the sea and away in the ship which had so soon been caught by the storm.

Such shape-shifting was familiar among the magicians of Egypt, though it seemed from Helen's words that only the gods practiced it in Greece, and that magic was hardly known in her country.

'Therefore, great Pharaoh,' begged Helen, 'protect me in honor here until my lord and love Menelaus comes to seek and claim me from you and do not let this evil prince carry me as a shameful captive to Troy.'

Helen wept, and the great red jewel she wore, the Star Stone which the goddess of love had given her, seemed to weep tears of blood as it trembled on her boson in the dazzling sunlight that feel between the columns.

Seti was much moved by her tale and he swore an oath to her, saying, 'By Amon-Ra, Father of Gods and Men, I swear that here in the Temple of Hathor you shall dwell with all honor until Menelaus comes for you. And I will send away this evil Prince of Troy without his treasure or his captive and if he strives to steal you again he shall meet his death, and any of his nation who come to Egypt seeking you stand in danger of death also.'

All things were done as Pharaoh Seti commanded. The Prince of Troy raged and threatened in vain. The Treasure he had stolen was taken from him and set in Pharaoh's treasure until Menelaus should come to claim it; and Paris was told that he must depart forthwith in his ship down the Nile before sunrise on the next day.

'I will depart indeed!' he shouted when Pharaoh's messenger brought him the royal command. 'But it will be up the river to resuce my wife from those who should keep her from me!'

Yet before the sun rose the Trojan ship was speeding down the river below Heliopolis, and ere the next sun rose it was out on the Great Green Sea, heading northwards towards Troy on the outskirts of the world.

All this came about very strangely, or so any of the Aquaiusha would have thought: but to the people of Egypt it was not at all out of the ordinary.

On the night before the Prince of Troy set sail, Pharaoh Seti's daughter Tausert knelt in prayer in the Temple of Hathro, for she was High Priestess of that goddess. As she knelt it seemed to her that the temple shook and a great light shone behind her. Turning, she beheld the shape of Thoth himself, the great god of wisdom and messenger of Amon-Ra.

'Fear not,' said Thoth as Tausert fell on her face before him. 'I come hither to work the will of the most high god Amon-Ra, father of us all and by his command you, who shall one day be Queen of Egypt, must learn of all that is performed this night so that you may bear witness of it in the days to come, when that king of Aquaiusha who is the true husband of Helen shall come to lead her home.'

'Know then that it is the will of Amon-Ra that the Aquaiusha, amongst whom he is worshipped by the name of Zeus, shall fight a great war for Helen which shall last for ten years and end only when the city of Troy lies in ruins. For the beauty of Helen shall it be fought, for an empty beauty, since here Helen remains until Menelaus comes. But this night I, whom the Aquaiusha name Hermes the Thrice Great, must draw forth the Ka, the double of Helen, the ghostly likeness of her that shall deceive all eyes and seem to Paris and to all at Troy to be none other than the real woman. For the Ka of Helen and not for Helen herself shall the great war of Troy be fought and the will of the Father of Gods and Men shall be accomplished.'

Then Thoth passed out of the shrine towards the cell where Helen dwelt. And presently the light shone in the shrine once more and Tausert sawa him pass through it followed by the Ka of Helen, so like Helen

herself that none could tell the difference. Thoth leading the way, they passed through the closed door of the
temple and so onwards through the night until they
reached where the ship lay at the quay-side below
Memphis. And there Thoth, thakking on the form of
Hermes by whivch Paris would know him, delivered
the Ka of Helen into his hands. And, rejoicing greatly,
Paris cast off the mooring ropes and set sail northwards
for Troy.

Yet Helen dwelt still in the Temple of Hathor at Memphis. And as the years passed most of the Egyptians forgot how she had come there, and many worshipped her
as Hathor come to earth in human form, and most
spoke of her as the Strange Hathor.

In time Seti died. His spirit went to dwell in the Hall of
Osiris and his body was laid to rest in the great tomb
below the Valley of Kings in Western Thebes. There
was then a time of trouble in Egypt when all of his sons
struggled for the throne. But at length, Set-Nakhte
wore the Double Crown and held the scourge and the
crook and his half-sister Tausert sat by his side as Queen
of Egypt.

Set-Nakhte did not reigh for long, and when he too was
gathered to Osiris, his son the third Rameses became
Pharaoh of Egypt.

All this while Helen had dwelt in the Temple of Hathor
at Memphis and, though it was nearly 20 years since
Paris had brought her to Egypt, she seemed scarcely to

have aged at all but was still more lovely than any other woman in the world.

Now both Seti and Set-Nakhte had faithfully observed the oath made to her. But young Rameses was of a different metal, and as soon as he became Pharaoh he declared that he would marry Helen and make her his Queen.

'She may be only a Princess of the Aquaiusha,' he declared. 'She may long ago have been the wife of one of the kings of that people but she is still the loveliest of women, and she shall be mine!'

In vain Queen Tausert tried to persuade him against so wicked a deed. 'I care nothing for what my father and grandfather may have sworn,' he cried. 'I have sworn no oath, except one, to marry Helen!'

'But,' urged Tausert, 'suppose her husband King Menelaus is still alive?'

This troubled Rameses a little, and he waited before marrying Helen until his chief magicians had looked into the matter for him.

While they were doing so, there came a shipwrecked sailor up the river to Membphis and knelt at the shrine of Hathor to pray for help. Tausert was still the High Priestess of Hathor, and now that her son was Pharaoh, she had returned to dwell in the Temple. So when she saw the sailor kneeling in the shrine, she went to ask him whence he came and why he had come to the

Temple of Hathor instead of that of Hershef, where strangers usually sought sanctuary.

'I come in obedience to a dream,' answered the man. 'Hermes, whom you call Thoth, visited me as I slept and asked me to seek the Strange Hathor in her temple at Memphis and tell my tale without hiding anything.'

'Speak on,' answered Tausert, 'and fear nothing. The Strange Hathor sits hidden in the shrine and hears all that you tell me.'

'Then know,' said the sailor, 'that I am Menelaus, King of Sparta. Troy fell several years ago, and since then I and my ships have been blown hither and thither about the seas. At length I am in my ship to the mouth of the River of Egypt, and with me was my wife the beautiful Helen, whom Paris stole and to rescue whom the war was fought. My other ships anchored behind the Island of Pharos, but I sailed into the mouth of the Nile, and there my ship was struck by a sudden storm of wind and wrecked on a little island.'

'We all escaped safely to the shore and sought shelter in some caves nearby. Helen and I were alone in one cave and when I awoke in the morning she had vanished. All day we searched for her, but there was no trace. She could not have left the island, for the river ran deep and fierce all round it, and we could only think that she had strayed too near the water's edge and been carried away by a crocodile.'

'I was in despair. To have fought for ten years at Troy to win back Helen; to have wandered on the sea for seven years trying to bring her home to Sparta and then to lose her like this seemed unbearable. I was tempted to fall upon my own sword and seek her in the fields of asphodel where Hades reigns, whom you call Osiris.'

'Then, as I lay mourning for my loss, Hermes appeared to me, *Do not despair, Menelaus, he said. All that has chanced is by the will of Zeus. Helen is not lost to you she was never found. In the morning a ship of the Egyptians will carry you to Memphis. There seek Helen in the Temple of the Strange Hathor. Enter the temple and tell your tale to the priestess there and you will find the true Helen.*'

'All this I have done. A ship came to the island the next day and carried us up the river to Memphis and here I kneel as Hermes bade me.'

'King of Sparta,' said Tausert solemnly, 'the will of Amon-Ra, whom you call Zeus, is accomplished; 17 years ago, in the days when the good god, my father, Seti Merneptah was Pharaoh, Paris the Prince of Troy was driven with his ship into the Nile, and Thoth the all-wise, whom you call Hermes, decreed that Helen should remain here in safety and honor until you came for her, and here she still dwells.'

'But Priestess,' gasped Menelaus, 'Helen went with Paris to Troy! We sacked Troy and I carried Helen away on my ship. She was with me until two days ago when she vanished from the island. How can she have been here ever since Paris stole her from my palace in Sparta?'

'By the will of Amon-Ra the Ka of Helen was drawn forth by Thoth and sent with Paris,' answered Tausert. 'For a double, a mere spirit form, did you of the Aquaiusha fight and Troy fall? Here is Helen!'

As she spoke, Tausert drew back the curtains of the shrine and Helen stepped forth with outstretched arms; beautiful Helen, untouched by years of siege and wandering, or by the unwished love of Paris.

Like a man in a dream Menelaus took Helen in his arms and held her as if to feel whether she were shadow or woman.

'Helen!' he murmured. 'Did you dwell here all these years while Paris carried a mere thing of air to Troy? Have we fought and died for a mere eidolon, a magic likeness, not a real woman? Truly the magic of the Egyptians is greater even than we have ever thought and in Greece they are spoken of as the wisest of all men!'

Then Helen said: 'My lord and my love, we are not safe yet. Although I have dwelt here all the years honored and unharmed, a great danger has come upon me suddenly. The new Pharaoh, Rameses, the son of this lady, my protectress Tausert, wishes to make me his wife and today he comes for his answer: whether I will be his willingly or by force.'

'This royal lady, Queen Tausert, does she favor the match?' asked Menelaus.

'So little,' replied Tausert, 'that I will do all in my power to help you both to escape from Egypt provided no harm comes to Rameses my son.'

then the three of them spoke together and devised a daring scheme. At noon that day came Rameses the Pharaoh to the Temple of Hathor to claim fair Helen as his bride. He found her clad in mourning garments with her hair hanging loose, while Menelaus, still ragged and unshaven as befitted a shipwrecked sailor, stood respect-fully at a little distance and Queen Tausert strove to comfort Helen.

'What has happened here?' asked Rameses.

'That for which you prayed, my son,' answered Tausert. 'This man is a messenger whom you should welcome. He was a sailor who came from Troy in the ship of Menelaus of Sparta, that prince of the Aquaiusha who was husband to Helen. The ship in which she sailed was wrecked on the island of Pharos, and Menelaus is dead.'

'Is this true, stranger?' asked Rameses.

'Oh, Pharaoh, life, health, strength be to you!' answered Menelaus, kneeling before him in the Egyptian manner. 'With my own eyes I saw him dashed on the rocks, and the waves carry his broken body out to sea.'

'Then, Helen, nothing stands between us!' cried Rameses.

'Only the memory of him who was my husband,' answered Helen.

'Your grief cannot be great after all these years.'

'Yet he was my husband, and a great king among my people the Greeks, and I would mourn him and pay funeral rites to his memory so that his spirit may be at rest and dwell in the land where Hades rules. Wherefore I beg you to let me honor him as a king should be honored though his body is lost in the deep sea.'

'That I grant willingly,' said Rameses. 'You have but to command, and all shall be done as you wish. I know nothing of the funeral customs of the Aquaiusha, so you must instruct me.'

'I must have a ship,' said Helen, 'well furnished with food and wine for the funeral feast, and a great bull to sacrifice to the spirit of my husband. And I must have treasures also; those which Paris stole long ago from my husband's palace when he carried me away. This sailor here and his companions in shipwreck should accompany me, for they know all that should be done, and it will take many men to perform the sacrifice. I must accompany them to speak the words and pour the last offering to my husband's spirit. All this must be done on the sea in which his body lies, for then only can his spirit find rest in the realm of Hades and only then can I be your bride.'

Because he was so eager to win Helen, Rameses agreed to all that she asked. A ship was loaded with the treasures that Seti had taken from Paris; the Greek sailors, Menelaus among them, brought the great sacrificial bull on board and took charge of it; Helen, wearing her mourning robes, stood in the prow of the ship, the sunlight flashing on the red Star Stone that she wore and the ship sailed swiftly down the Nile and out to the sea near Canopus.

But next day there came a messenger, stained with brine and the dust of travel, and knelt before Rameses, crying, 'Oh, Pharaoh life, health, strength be to you! That sailor of the Aquaiusha who came with the death of Menelaus was none other than Menelaus himself! When the ship was well out of the Great Green Sea beyond Canopus, the Aquaiusha sacrificed the bull indeed, but to the sea god to give them a safe passage back to Greece. Then they seized us to Egypt who were on the ship and cast us into the sea, bidding us swim back to Memphis and tell you, Oh Pharaoh, that the will of Amon-Ra and of Thoth was accomplished and Helen, safe both from Paris the Trojan and from you, was on her way back to Sparta with her lawful husband, Menelaus.'

Now in his anger and disappointment Rameses wished to kill Tausert his mother, for he realized that she had known about Menelaus and had helped to rob him of

Helen. But that night ibis-headed Thoth appeared to him and said, *Pharaoh Rameses, all these strange happenings have been by the will of Amon-Ra the god and father of all Pharaohs. By his will, Helen was brought to Egypt; at his command I drew forth her Ka and sent it to Paris, to deceive him and all the Aquaiusha and the Peoples of the Sea; and he brought it about that Helen should be restored to her husband and sent to her home with him and with the treasures that Paris stole.'*

Then Pharaoh Rameses bowed his head to the will of Amon-Ra and heaped greater honors yet upon his mother, Queen Tausert, High Priestess of Hathor."

Chapter 16:
The Adventures of Sinuhe

"Despite everything he had done to unite Egypt and bring peace and prosperity to her after years of civil war, Pharaoh Amen-em-het went in constant danger from plots to murder him, created by one lord or another, who want to take control of his throne.

Fearing that one of these plots might prove to be successful, and knowing that if one of the lords tried to take the throne that it would plunge Egypt into a civil war once more, Amen-em-het promoted his son Sen-Usert to be his a co-ruler with him, so that he could take over as Pharaoh immediately if something happened to him. This could help to put down any uprising or rebellion that could occur.

Amen-em-het's wisdom was proven ten years later when one of the murder attempts proves successful. Sen-Usert was abroad when his father died, leading an army against Temeh in Libya. He had defeated the enemy and was returning to Egypt with many captives and treasures, when a messenger arrived at night. It was obvious that he was bearing some important news for the Prince.

Among Sen-Usert's chosen bodyguard of Royal Companions was a young warrior known as Sinuhe who knew a lot more than he should have about the plot against Amen-em-het. When he saw the messengers, Sinuhe guessed that they must have news about what had happened at Thebes, and he crept silently up to the back of the royal pavilion and stood there as if on guard. As he stood there, he took the dagger and made a slit in the material where it was stretched over one of the posts so that he could hear everything that was being said inside.

Sinuhe could hear the message that was being told to Sen-Usert about the death of his father, and that he was now Pharaoh. 'You must ride for Thebes at once,' the messenger said. 'Do not tell the army what has happened, but set out immediately with only the Royal Companions. Other messengers have gone to your faithful governors throughout Egypt commanding them to hide the news of the death of Pharaoh Amen-em-het from the people until Pharaoh Sen-Usert, life, health, strength be to him, is proclaimed in Thebes.'

When Sinuhe heard all of this, he was immediately filled with fear. If he traveled to Memphis with Sen-Usert and the Royal Companions his part in the murder plot for Amen-em-het may be uncovered. If he asked to stay behind with the army, he might be suspected, and Sen-Usert would certainly notice that he had been spying and overhead the secret news.

It is possible that none of these things could have happened, but Sinuhe was seized with such panic that he slipped quietly out of the camp to wait until he saw which way the army was marching. He then crept down and made his way south along the edge of the desert, trying to avoid the villages and towns. When he reached the area where the Nile started to branch out into the many streams of the Delta, he was in more danger of being seen. One man whom he unexpectedly ran into turned and fled, thinking that he was a bandit. He reach a district of islands and high reeds that evening, which must have been somewhere near where the modern city of Cairo now stands.

It was here that he found an old boat without oars or rudder, and as the wind was blowing from the west, he boarded the boat and drifted downstream towards Heliopolis, but reached the eastern bank of the Nile a mile or so outside of town.

He then continued on his way, crossing over the isthmus Suez near the Bitter Lakes and traveling by night across the frontier and into the Desert of Sinai. It was here that he nearly died of thirst, and indeed had given up all hope and laid down never to rise again, but he heard the lowing of cattle.

He started out creeping on his hand and knees because he was so weak. Sinuhe came to a camp of Asiatic nomad. The sheikh of the tribe recognized him as an Egyptian and guessed by his appearance that he was a man of importance. So he took care of him, feeding him some milk and water until he was strong enough to consume more solid food.

After this, Sinude was able to make to the ancient city of Byblos in Syria without any other problems. This was where Egyptians had always been welcome since the great temple had been built on the spot where Isis found the body of Osiris in the column of Kin Malcander's palace.

He stayed in this place for some time, and then journeyed further east to the great valley beyond the Lebanon range where King Ammi=enshi ruled the land which was then called Retenu. Ammi-enshi welcomed him, saying, 'Come and dwell in my country. I have other men of Egypt who serve me, and you will at least hear your native language in this place. Moreover, it seems to me that you must have been a man of some importance in Egypt. Therefore, tell me why you have left your home. What news is there from the court of Pharaoh?'

Sinuhe replied by saying, 'Pharaoh Amen-em-het has departed to dwell beyond the horizon. He has been taken up to the place of the gods, and I fled, fearing civil war in Egypt and danger to those who had been near to Pharaoh. I left Egypt for no other reason but this. I was faithful to Pharaoh and no evil was spoken against me. Yet I think that some god must have guided me and led me hither.'

'I have gotten word from Egypt since you left it,' said Ammi-enshi. 'The new Pharaoh is Sen-Usert the son of Amen-em-het. He has taken his place upon the throne of the Two Lands, he has set the Double Crown of Upper and Lower Egypt upon his head, his hands hold the scourge and the crook. There has been no rebellion yet in Egypt, but do you think that war will come?'

Sinuhe quickly realized that Ammi-enshi was asking his advice as to whether it was safe to rebel against the rule of Egypt and seek to make Retenu an independent country outside of the Egyptian Empire, and he replied, 'If Sen-Usert is now Pharaoh, and all in Egypt are faithful to him, there will be no danger of rebellion or civil war. Sen-Usert is a god upon earth, a general without an equal. It was he who led the army against the Libyans of Temeh ad subdued them victoriously. He is a Pharaoh who will extend the frontiers of Egypt's empire. He will send his armies south into Nubia and east into Asia. Therefore, my advice to you is that you send messengers to kiss the ground before him. Let him know of your loyalty, for he will not fail to do good to all lands that are true to him.'

King Ammi-enshi replied with, 'How happy Egypt must be under such a strong and great Pharaoh. I will do even as you advise, but as for you, stay here with me and command my armies, and I will make you great.'

From then on, Sinuhe prospered in the land of Retenu. He married the eldest daughter of the King and was given a palace to live in upon an estate where all good things grew in abundance. He had groves of fig trees and vineyards where grapes grew so thickly that wine was more plentiful than water. There were rich fields of barley and wheat, and pastures where the cattle grew fat. Never did Sinuhe know any shortage of roast meats, either beef or chickens from his lands, or the wild things which he hunted with his hounds on the lower slopes of Mount Lebanon.

Sinuhe did not get all of this greatness for nothing. As commander of Ammi-enshi's army he made war on neighboring tribes and people who tried to invade Retenu from the north and east. In all of these ventures he proved to be successful, slaying the enemy with his strong arm and unerring arrows, carrying off the inhabitants as slaves and bringing back great droves of cattle to swell the royal herds.

With all of his help, King Ammi-enshi grew to love him as if he were his son, and planned on making him next in succession to the throne by right of his wife, the Princess Royal. It seemed that either the King Retenu had no sons or else the throne descended in the female line.

Not everybody in Retenu were pleased with the idea of being ruled in days to come by a foreigner, and there was a murmur of rebellion headed by a certain champion who was the strongest man and most famous warrior in the country, and against whom no one had been able to stand in battle.

When King Ammi-enshi heard of this, it troubled his heart and sent for Sinuhe, telling him, 'Do you know this man? Have you any secret that he was discovered?'

Sinuhe replied, 'My lord, I have never seen him. I have never entered his house. He comes against me out of jealousy and, if it pleases you, I will meet him in battle. Either his is a braggart who wishes to seize both my property and power, or else he is like a wild bull who wishes to gore the tame bull and add his cows to his own herd. He could simply be like a bull that can bear no other bull to be thought stronger or fiercer than he.'

The duel was the arranged. It was to take place before a great gathering of the people or Retenu, in the presence of the King himself. All night long Sinuhe practiced with his weapons, testing his bow and sharpening his javelins. A the break of day, he came to the battle field, and the people applauded him, crying, 'Can there be any fighting man greater than Sinuhe?'

But when the challenger came striding out from among his followers, the crow fell silent because he was a mighty man indeed. He began the battle, shooting at Sinuhe was his arrows, and hurling his javelins. But Sinuhe was quick footed and had sharp eyes, and he dodged them all or turned them harmlessly away with his shield.

Then he got ready to attack the challenge, who came rushing on him waving a might battle-axe above his head. Sinuhe shot an arrow, and the champion turned it with his shield. Then Sinuhe hurled a javelin so swiftly that the champion had not time to ward it off, but was struck in the neck by it, stumbled and fell upon his face.

The battle-axe flew out of his hand. Sinuhe seized hold of it and smote off his rival's head with a single blow.

All of the people of Retenu cheered him on, and the King caught him in his arms and embraced him, crying, 'Surely here is the worthiest man in all of the land to rule with me!'

So Sinuhe became the greatest lord in Retenu after Ammi-enshi, and ruled the land with him for many years, and became King after him when he died. But as he grew older, Sinuhe began to long for his homeland, and a great desire came upon him to see Egypt once more before he died and be laid to rest at last in a rock tomb at Thebes.

Pharaoh Sen-Usert knew that the new King of Retenu was that Sinuhe who had been his Royal Companion in the days of Amen-em-het. He had sent letters to him as to a loyal subject, and Sinuhe had replied as a loyal subject should.

He wrote begging that be forgiven for leaving the royal service at such a time of uncertainty after Amen-em-het's death, and asked if he could return to Egypt to spend his old age there.

Sen-Usert wrote back at once and told him to come live in the Royal Palace as a great lord and trusted adviser, and he ended his letter saying, 'Return to Egypt to look againt upon the land where you were born and the palace where you served me so faithfully in the days before

Osiris took to himself my father the good god Amen-em-het. You are now growing old, you are no longer a young man bent upon adventures. Look forward to the day of your burial. Do not let death come upon you far away among the Asiatic. Live with me in Egypt, and when that day comes you shall be laid to rest at Western Thebes in a mummy case of rich gold with your face inlaid upon it in lapis lazuli. A sledge drawn by oxen shall bring you to your tomb while the singers go in front and the dancers follow behind until you come to the door of your sepulcher. That shall be made for you in the midst of the royal tombs where princes and viziers lie. The walls will be painted with all the wisdom of the dead so that you Ba shall pass safely into the Duat. Rich treasures and plentiful offering shall be set in your tomb so that your Ka may feast upon them until the day comes when Osiris shall return to earth. Come quickly, for you grow old and you know not when you may die. It is not right that a noble of Egypt should be laid in the earth wrapped in a sheepskin like a mere Asiatic. Come quickly, for you have roamed too long.'

Sinuhe rejoiced when he got this letter. He quickly made arrangements to hand over the rule of Retenu with all his possessions to his eldest son. Then he set out for Egypt attended by a small party of his chose followers.

Once they got to the borders of Egypt, he was met by an embassy from the Pharaoh who welcomed him warmly and made much of the lords of Retenu who had come with him. At the Nile, a ship was waiting for him, and Sinuhe was taken up the river in a great state and comfort to the palace of Pharaoh. Once he was taken into the royal presence he prostrated himself on the ground before the throne and laid there as if he were dead.

Then, Pharaoh Sen-Usert, said kindly, 'Lift him up and let him speak. Sinuhe, you have arrived at your home, you have ceased to wander in foreign lands and come back in honorable old age so that when the time comes you may be laid to rest in a fine tomb at Western Thebes and not thrust into the ground by Asiatic barbarians. See, I greet you by name. Welcome, Sinuhe!'

Then Sinuhe rose and stood before Sen-Usert with downcast eyes and said, 'Behold, I stand before you and my life is yours to do with as you will.'

Pharaoh stepped down from his throne and took Sinuhe by the hand. He led him to the Queen and said to her laughingly, 'See, here is Sinuhe, dressed like a wild Asiatic of the desert.'

All of the royal children came to great him as well, and Pharaoh uttered his decree, 'I make Sinuhe a Companion of Pharaoh, a great lord of the Court. I give him such lands and riches as becomes such a one, those that he forfeited when he fled from Egypt long ago, and more than he lost, to welcome him on his return and show how happy we are to have him with us once more.'

And so Sinuhe became a great man in Egypt and a close friend of the Pharaoh from whom he had fled in a moment of panic. He gave lavish care to the carving and decorating of his tomb, and caused all the story of his adventures to be written on it, and also to be copied out and kept in the archives. And when he died, he was laid to rest with all honor.

He tomb has never been discovered, but the account of his adventures has come to us, for it was a favorite tale in Ancient Egypt and was written down many times and red for hundreds of years after his passing."

Chapter 17: The Two Brothers

"There once was two brothers. These brothers were the sons of the same father and the same mother. Anpu was the name of the elder, and the younger boy was called Bata. Anpu had a house of his own, and he had a wife. His brother lived with him as if he were his son, and made garments for him. It was Bata who drove the oxen to the field. He was the one who ploughed the land, and it was he who harvested the grain. He labored continually upon his brother's farm, and his equal was not to be found in the land of Egypt. He was imbued with the spirit of a god.

The brothers continued to live together in this way, and many days went by. Every morning, the younger boy would head out with the oxen and when evening came, he would drive them again to the cowshed, carrying upon his back a heavy burden of fodder which he gave to the animals to eat. He would then bring milk and herbs in for Anpu and his wife. While the two would eat and drink together in the house, Bata would rest in the cowshed with the cattle and he would sleep with them as well.

When day would break, and the land grew bright once more, the younger brother would be the first one up, and he would bake bread for Anpu and carried his own portion out to the field and would eat it there. As he followed the oxen he heard and he understood their speech. They would say, 'Yonder is sweet herbage,' and he would drive them to the area that they had chosen, and once there, they were very happy. They were indeed noble animals, and they increased greatly.

Once the time for ploughing arrived, Anpu would speak to Bata and say, 'Now get the team of oxen ready because the Nile flood is past and the land may be broken up. We shall begin to plough tomorrow, so carry seeds to the field that we can sow it.'

Bata did as Anpu asked. When the next day dawned, and the land grew bright, the two brothers labored in the field together, and they were well pleased with the work that they accomplished. Several days went past in this way, and it just so happened that on an afternoon, the seeds were all planted and they had finished their day's tasks.

Anpu then told his younger brother, 'Quickly go to the granary and get us some more seeds.'

Bata ran towards the house and went in. He saw his brother's wife sitting upon a mat, languidly combing her hair.

'Get up,' he said, 'and get the corn for me so that I can quickly return to the fields with it. Delay me not.'

The women did not move and simply replied, 'Go yourself and open the storeroom. Take whatever you want. If I were to get up for you, my hair would fall into disorder.'

Bata opened the storeroom and went inside. He took a large basket and poured a large amount of seeds into it. Then he came back out carrying the basket through the house.

The women looked up and said, 'What is the weight of that great burden of yours?'

Bata replied, 'There are two measures of barley and three of wheat. I carry five measures of seed altogether on my shoulders.'

'Your strength is great indeed,' the woman sighed, 'Ah, I admire and contemplate you every day.'

Her heart was moved towards him, and she stood up saying, 'Linger here with me. I will clothe you in fine garments.'

This made Bata angry, and he replied, 'I see you as my mother, and my brother is like a father to me. You have spoken evil words, and I desire not to hear them again, nor will I repeat those words you have just said to anybody else.'

He left quickly with his seeds and ran back to the field, where he continued working. Once evening came around, Anpu returned home and Bata prepared to follow after him. The elder brother went into his house and found his wife lying there, and it seemed as though she had been hurt by some evildoer. She did not give him water to wash his hands, as was her custom. She also didn't light the lamp. The house was completely dark. She moaned where she laid, as if she were sick, and her garments were laid out beside her.

'Who has been here?' Anpu asked.

The women replied, 'No one came here except for your younger brother. He spoke evil words to me, and I asked him, *am I not as a mother, and is not your elder brother like a father to you*? Then he became very angry and he struck me until I promised that I would not tell you. If you allow him to live, I will surely die.'

The elder brother immediately became angry at his brother. He sharpened his dagger and went out and stood behind the door of the cowshed with the sole purpose of slaying the young Bata when he arrived.

The sun had already set when Bata drove the oxen into the cowshed, carrying the herbs and fodder on his back, and in one hand a vessel of milk, as was his customer every evening. The first ox walked into the shed, and then said to Bata, 'Beware, for your elder brother is standing behind the door. In his hand is a dagger, and he wants to kill you. Do not come in here.'

Bata heard and understood what the animal had said. Then the second ox walked into the shed and went to its stall, and spoke similar words of warning, saying, 'Take speedy flight.'

Bata peeked into the shed door, and he saw the legs of his brother, who was standing there with a dagger in his hand. He at once threw down everything he was carrying and made a quick escape. Anpu rushed after him with the sharp dagger.

In his distress, the younger brother cried out to the sun god Ra, and said, 'Blessed lord, you are the one who could distinguish between what was true and what was false.'

The god heard Bata's cry with compassion, and turned round. He created a wide stream to flow between the two brothers, and, behold, it was full of crocodiles. Then, Anpu and Bata stood face to face, one was on the right bank and the other on the left. The elder brother smacked his hands together with anguish because he could not slay his brother.

Bata called out to Anpu, and said, 'Stay where you are until the earth is made bright once more. When Ra, the sun god, rises up, I shall reveal in his presence all that I know, and he shall judge between us, discerning what is false and what is true. Know that I can't stay with you any longer, for I have to go into the fair region of the flowering acacia.'

When the sun came up, and the sun god Ra appeared in all of his glory, the two brothers stood gazing upon each other across the stream of crocodiles. The younger brother spoke to the elder brother, and said, 'Why did you come after me, desiring to kill me with treachery without me getting to speak for myself? Am I not you younger brother, and have you not been a father and your wife a mother to me? Hear and know now that when I rushed in to get seeds you wife asked me to stay with her, but I see that this has been told to you in a different manner.'

So Bata told his brother what was true in regards to his wife. Then he called to witness the sun god and said, 'Great was you wickedness in wanting to murder me by treachery.' As he spoke, he cut off a piece of his flesh and flung it into the stream, where it was eaten by a fish. He sank, fainting upon the bank.

Anpu was stricken with anguish, tears running down his eyes. He wanted to be beside his brother on the other bank of the stream of crocodiles.

Bata spoke once more, 'Certainly, you did desire an evil thing, but if want you want to do now is good, I will instruct you on what you should do. Return to your home and tend to your oxen, for know now that I will not live with you any longer, but must depart to the fair region of the flowering acacia. What you shall do is to come to find me when I need your help, for my soul will leave my body and will live in the highest blossom of the acacia. When the tree is cut down, my soul will fall to the ground. There you can look for it, even if you have to look for seven years for you shall find it if you desire to. You must then place it into a vessel of water, and I will come to life again and reveal all that has happened and what will happen after that. When time comes to set forth on this quest, see that the beer given to you will bubble, and the wine will have a foul smell. These will be your signs.'

Then Bata took off, and he went into the valley of the flowering acacia, which was across the ocean. He older brother returned home. He lamented, throwing dust upon his head. He killed his wife and threw her to the dogs, and abandoned himself to mourn for the loss of his brother.

Many days past, and Bata reached, after some time, the valley of the flowering acacia. He lived there along and hunted wild beasts. Once evening came, he laid down to rest below the acacia, in whose highest blossom his soul was concealed. In time, he built a place to live, and he filled the home with everything that he wanted.

Now it so happened that on a day when he went forth, he met the nine gods, who were surveying the enter land. They spoke one to another and then asked for Bata why he had forsaken his home because of his brother's wife, for she had since been slain. 'Return again,' they said to him, 'for you did reveal to your elder brother the truth of what happen to you.'

They took pity on the boy, and Ra spoke, 'Create a bride for Bata, so that he may not be along.' Then the god Khnumu created a wife whose body was more beautiful than any other woman's in the land because she had been filled with divinity.

Then the seven Hathors came and gazed upon her. In a single voice they said, 'She will surely die a speedy death.'

Bata loved her dearly. Every day she stayed in his house while he hunted wild beasts, and he carried them home and laid them at her feet. He warned her every day with the same messae, 'Do not go outside, lest the sea may come up and carry you away. I could not rescue you from the sea spirit, against whom I am as weak as you are because my soul is concealed in the highest blossom of the flowering acacia. If another should fine my soul, I will have to fight for it.'

With that, he opened his whole heart to her and revealed his secrets.

Several days past. Then on a morning when Bata had gone out to hunt, as was his custom, his wife left the house to walk below the acacia which was near the house. Suddenly, the sea spirit saw her in all of her beauty and caused his waves to pursue her. She quickly fled and returned to the house, and then the sea spirit sang to the acacia, 'Oh, would she were mine.'

The acacia heard and cast to the sea spirit a lock of the wife's hair. The sea carried it away towards the land of Egypt and to the place where the washers of the king cleansed the royal garments.

Sweet was the fragrance of the lock of hair, and it perfumed the linen of the king. There were disputes among the washers because the royal garments smelled of ointment, nor could anyone discover the secret of the smell. The king criticized them.

Then was the heart of the chief washer in sore distress because of the words that were spoken each day to him in regards to this matter. He went down to the seashore. He stood at the place opposite of the floating lock of hair, and he saw it at length and had it brought to him. Sweet was its fragrance, and he quickly took it to the king.

Then the king called his scribes in, and they said, 'Behold, this is a lock of hair from the divine daughter of Ra, and it is gifted to you from a distant land. Command now that messengers be sent abroad to look for her. Let many men go with the one who is sent to the valley of the flowering acacia so that they may bring the woman to you.'

The replied, and said, 'Wise are your words, and they are pleasant to me.'

His messengers were sent abroad to all of the lands. But those who were sent to the valley of the flowering acacia never returned because Bata slew them all. The king never found how what happened to them.

Then the king sent our more messengers and many soldiers so that the girl could be brought to him. He also sent a women, and she was give rare ornaments, and the wife of Bata came back with her.

There was much rejoicing throughout the land of Egypt. Dearly did the king love the divine girl, and he honored her because of her beauty. He prevailed upon her to reveal the secrets of her husband, and then the king said, 'Let the acacia be cut down and splintered into pieces.'

Workmen and warriors were sent out, and they reached the acacia. The severed from it the highest blossom, in which the soul of Bata was concealed. The petals were scattered all around, and Bata dropped down dead. A new day dawned, and the land grew bright. The acacia was then cut down.

Meanwhile, Anpu, Bata's elder brother, went into his house and sat down and washed his hands. He was given beer to drink, and it bubbled, and the wine had a foul smell.

He grabbed his staff and put on his shoes and garments, and then he armed himself for his journey. He departed into the valley of the flowering acacia.

When he reached the house of Bata, he found the young man lying dead upon a mat. He bitterly wept because of his brother's death. But he quickly went out to search for the soul of his brother in the place where, below the flowering acacia, Bata was accustomed to lie down and rest during the evening. For three years he continued to search for it, and when the fourth year came, his heart yearned greatly to return to the land of Egypt. At length, he said, 'I shall depart at dawn tomorrow.'

A new day came, and the land grew bright. He looked over the ground once more at the place of the acacia for his brother's soul. The time was spent do just that. In the evening, he continued on his quest, and he found a seed. He carried the seed to the house and it turned out to be the soul of his brother. He dropped the seed into a vessel filled with cold water and sat down as was his evening custom.

Night came, and the soul absorbed the water. The limbs of Bata quivered and his eyes opened and gazed upon his elder brother, but his heart was without feeling. Then Anpu raised the vessel that help the soul to the lips of Bata, and he drank the water. His soul then returned to its rightful place, and Bata was as he had been before.

The brothers embraced and spoke to one another. Bata said, 'Now I must become a mighty bull with every scared mark. None will know my secret. You will ride upon my back, and when the day breaks, I will be at the palace where my wife is. To her I must speak. Lead me before the king, and you shall find favor in his eyes. The people will wonder when thee see me, and shout welcome. But you must go back to your own home.'

A new day dawned, and the land grew bright. Bata was a bull, and Anpu sat upon his back, and they drew closer to the royal dwelling. The king was made glad, and said, 'This is indeed a miracle.' Everybody rejoiced throughout the land. Silver and gold were given to the elder brother, and he returned back to his own him and waited there.

In time, the sacred bull stood in a holy place, and beautiful wife was there. Bata spoke to her, and said, 'Look upon me where I sand for I still live.'

Then the women replied, 'And who are you?'

The bull replied, 'Truly, I am Bata. It was you who caused the acacia to be cut down. It was you who did reveal to the Pharaoh that my soul had been living in the highest blossom so that it could be destroyed and I might cease to be. But, behold, I live on, and I am now a sacred bull.'

The woman trembled. Fear took over her heart when Bata spoke to her in this manner. She at once left the holy place. It just so happened that the king sat beside her at the feast and made merry, for he loved her dearly. She said, 'Promise before the god that you will do what I ask of you.'

His majesty took a vow to grant her the wish of her heart, and she said, 'It is my desire to eat the liver of the sacred bull, for he is nothing to you.'

The king was filled with sorrow, and his heart was troubled because of the words she said. A new day dawned, and the land grew bright. The king commanded that the bull be offered up as a sacrifice.

One of the king's chief servants went out, and when the bull was held high on the shoulders of the people, he cut its neck and it cast two drops of blood towards the gate of the palace, and one drop fell upon the right side and one upon the left. There grew up in the night two stately Persea trees from where the drops of blood fell.

A day came when his majesty rode forth in his golden chariot. He wore a collar of lapis lazuli, and around his neck was a garland of flowers. The wife was with him, and he caused her to stand below one of the trees, and it whispered to her, 'You false women, I am still alive. Behold, I am Bata, whom you tried to wrong. It was you who did cause the acacia to be cut down. It was you who caused the sacred bull to be slain so that I might cease to be.'

Several days past, and the woman sat with the king at the feast, and he loved her dearly. She said, 'Promise now before the god that you will do what I ask of you.'

His majesty made a vow of promised, and she said, 'If is my desire that the Persea trees be cut down so that two fair seats may be made of them.'

As she wanted, so was it done. The king commanded that the trees be cut down by a skilled workman, and the fair woman went out to watch them. As she stood there, a small chip of wood entered her mouth, and she swallowed it.

After several days, she gave birth to a son, and he was taken to the king, and he said, 'To you a son is given.' A nurse and servants were appoint to care for the baby. There was great rejoicing throughout the land when the time came to name the wife's son. The king was happy, and from then on, he loved the child and appointed him the Prince of Ethiopia.

Many days went past, and then the king chose him to be the heir to the kingdom. In time, his majesty grew old, and he died. His soul then flew off to the heavens.

The new king, Bata, then said, 'Summon before me the great men of my court so that I may new reveal to them all that has happened to me and the truth concerning the queen.'

His wife was then brought before him. He revealed himself to her, and she was judged before the great men, and they confirmed the sentence. Then Anpu was summoned before His Majesty, and he was chosen to be the royal heir. When Bata had reigned for 30 years, he came to his death, and on the day of his burial, his elder brother stood in his place."

Chapter 18: The Tale of the Fugitive Prince

"King Khufu sat to hear tales told by his sons regarding the wonders of other days and the doings of magicians. The Prince Khafra stood before him and related the ancient story of the wax crocodile.

Once upon a time a Pharaoh went towards the temple of the god Ptah. His counselors and servants accompanied him. It chanced that he paid a visit to the villa of the chief scribe, behind which there was a garden with a stately summer house and a broad artificial lake. Among those who followed Pharaoh was a handsome youth, and the scribe's wife beheld him with love. Soon afterwards she sent gifts to him, and they had secret meetings. They spent a day in the summer house, and feasted there, and in the evening the youth bathed in the lake. The chief butler then went to his master and informed him what had come to pass.

The scribe bade the servant to bring a certain magic box, and when he received it he made a small wax crocodile, over which he muttered a spell. He placed it in the hands of the butler, saying, 'Cast this image into the lake behind the youth when next he bathes himself.'

On another day, when the scribe dwelt with Pharaoh, the lovers were together in the summer house, and at eventide the youth went into the lake. The butler stole through the garden, and stealthily he cast into the water the wax image, which was immediately given life. It became a great crocodile that seized the youth suddenly and took him away.

Seven days passed, and then the scribe spoke to the Pharaoh regarding the wonder which had been done, and made request that His Majesty should accompany him to his villa. The Pharaoh did so, and when they both stood beside the lake in the garden the scribe spoke magic words, bidding the crocodile to appear. As he commanded, so did it do. The great reptile came out of the water carrying the youth in its jaws.

The scribe said, 'Look, it will do whatever I command to be done.'

Said the Pharaoh, 'Ask the crocodile to return at once to the lake.'

In time, he did that, the scribe touched it, and immediately it became a small image of wax again. The Pharaoh was filled with wonder, and the scribe related unto him all that had happened, while the youth stood waiting.

Said His Majesty to the crocodile, 'Seize the wrongdoer.' The wax image was again given life, and, clutching the youth, leaped into the lake and disappeared. Nor was it ever seen after that.

Then Pharaoh gave command that the wife of the scribe should be seized. On the north side of the house she was bound to a stake and burned alive, and what remained of her was thrown into the Nile.

And that was the tale told by Khafra. Khufu was well pleased, and called for offerings of food and refreshment to be placed in the tombs of the Pharaoh and his wise servant.

Prince Khafra stood before His Majesty, and said, 'I will relate a marvel which happened in the days of King Sneferu, thy father.' Then he told the story of the green jewel.

Sneferu was one day disconsolate and weary. He wandered about the palace with desire to be cheered, nor was there anything that could take the gloom from his mind. He caused his chief scribe to be brought before him, and said, 'I would love to have entertainment, but cannot find any in this place.'

The scribe said, 'Thy Majesty should go boating on the lake, and let the rowers be the prettiest girls in your harem. It will delight your heart to see them splashing the water where the birds dive and to gaze upon the green shores and the flowers and trees. I myself will go with you.'

The king consented, and twenty virgins who were fair to behold went into the boat, and they rowed with oars of ebony which were decorated with gold. His Majesty took pleasure in the outing, and the gloom passed from his heart as the boat went to and fro, and the girls sang together with sweet voices.

It chanced, as they were turning round, an oar handle brushed against the hair of the girl who was steering, and shook from it a green jewel, which fell into the water. She lifted up her oar and stopped singing, and the others grew silent and ceased rowing.

Senefru said, 'Do not pause; let us go on still farther.'

The girls replied, 'She who steers has lifted her oar.'

Said Sneferu to her, 'Why have you lifted your oar?'

'Alas, I have lost my green jewel she said it has fallen into the lake.'

Sneferu said, 'I will give you another; let us go on.'

The girl pouted and replied, 'I would rather have my own green jewel again than any other.'

His Majesty said to the chief scribe, 'I am given great enjoyment by this novelty; indeed my mind is much refreshed as the girls row me up and down the lake. Now one of them has lost her green jewel, which has dropped into the water, and she wants it back again and will not have another to replace it.'

The chief scribe at once muttered a spell. Then by reason of his magic words the waters of the lake were divided like a lane. He went down and found the green jewel which the girl had lost, and came back with it to her. When he did that, he again uttered words of power, and the waters came together as they were before.

The king was well pleased, and when he had full enjoyment with the rowing upon the lake he returned to the palace. He gave gifts to the chief scribe, and everyone wondered at the marvel which he had accomplished.

Such was Khafra's tale of the green jewel, and King Khufu commanded that offerings should be laid in the tombs of Sneferu and his chief scribe, who was a great magician.

Next Prince Hordadef stood before the king, and he said, 'Your Majesty has heard tales regarding the wonders performed by magicians in other days, but I can bring forth a worker of marvels who now lives in the kingdom.'

King Khufu said, 'And who is he, my son?'

'His name is Dedi,' answered Prince Hordadef. 'He is a very old man, for his years are 110. Each day he eats a joint of beef and five hundred loaves of bread, and drinks a hundred jugs of beer. He can smite off the head of a living creature and restore it again. He can make a lion follow him; and he knows the secrets of the habitation of the god Thoth, which Your Majesty has desired to know so that you may design the chambers of your pyramid.'

King Khufu said, 'Go now and find this man for me, Hordadef.'

The prince went down to the Nile, boarded a boat, and sailed southward until he reached the town called Dedsnefru, where Dedi had his dwelling. He went ashore, and was carried in his chair of state towards the magician, who was found lying at his door. When Dedi was awakened, the king's son saluted him and bade him not to rise up because of his years. The prince said, 'My royal father desires to honor you, and will provide for you a tomb among your people.'

Dedi blessed the prince and the king with thankfulness, and he said to Hordadef: 'Greatness be yours. May your Ka have victory over the powers of evil, and may your Khu follow the path which leads to Paradise.'

Hordadef assisted Dedi to rise up, and took his arm to help him towards the ship. He sailed away with the prince, and in another ship were his assistants and his magic books.

'Health and strength and plenty be yours,' said Hordadef, when he again stood before his royal father King Khufu. 'I have come down stream with Dedi, the great magician.'

His Majesty was well pleased, and said, 'Let the man be brought into my presence.'

Dedi came and saluted the king, who said, 'Why have I not seen you before?'

'He that is called cometh,' answered the old man. 'You have sent for me and I am here.'

'It is told,' King Khufu said, 'that you can restore the head that is taken from a live creature.'

'I can indeed, Your Majesty,' answered Dedi.

The king said, 'Then let a prisoner be brought forth and decapitated.'

'I would rather it were not a man,' said Dedi. 'I do not deal even with cattle in such a manner.'

A duck was brought forth and its head was cut off, and the head was thrown to the right and the body to the left. Dedi spoke magic words. Then the head and the body came together, and the duck rose up and quacked loudly. The same was done with a goose.

King Khufu then caused a cow to be brought in, and its head was cut off. Dedi restored the animal to life again, and caused it to follow him.

His Majesty then spoke to the magician and said, 'It is told that you possess the secrets of the dwelling of the god Thoth.'

Dedi answered, 'I do not possess them, but I know where they are concealed, and that is within a temple chamber at Heliopolis. There the plans are kept in a box, but it is no insignificant person who shall bring them to Your Majesty.'

'I would fain know who will deliver them unto me,' King Khufu said.

Dedi prophesied that three sons would be born to Rud-dedit, wife of the chief priest of Ra. The eldest would become chief priest at Heliopolis and would possess the plans. He and his brothers would one day sit upon the throne and rule over all the land.

King Khufu's heart was filled with gloom and alarm when he heard the prophetic words of the great magician.

Dedi then said, 'What are your thoughts, O King? Behold your son will reign after you, and then his son. But next one of these children will follow.'

King Khufu was silent. Then he spoke and asked, 'When shall these children be born?'

Dedi informed His Majesty, who said, 'I will visit the temple of Ra at that time.'

Dedi was honoured by His Majesty, and thereafter lived in the house of the Prince Hordadef. He was given daily for his portion an ox, a thousand loaves of bread, a hundred jugs of beer, and a hundred bunches of onions.

The day came when the sons of the woman Rud-dedit were to be born. Then the high priest of Ra, her husband, prayed to the goddess Isis and her sister Nephtys; to Meskhent, goddess of birth; and to the frog goddess Hekt; and to the creator god Khnumu, who gives the breath of life. These he entreated to have care of the three babes who were to become three kings of Egypt, one after the other.

The deities heard him. Then came the goddesses as dancing girls, who went about the land, and the god Khnumu followed them as their burden bearer. When they reached the door of the high priest's dwelling they danced before him. He entreated them to enter, and they did according to his desire, and shut themselves in the room with the woman Rud-dedit.

Isis called the first child who was born Userkaf, and said, 'Let no evil be done by him.' The goddess Meskhent prophesied that he would become King of Egypt. Khnumu, the creator god, gave the child strength.

The second babe was named Sahura by the goddess Isis. Meskhent prophesied that he also would become a king. Khnumu gave him his strength.

The third was called Kaka. Meskhent said, 'He shall also be a king,' and Khnumu gave him strength.

Ere the dancing girls took their departure the high priest gave a measure of barley to their burden bearer, and Khnumu carried it away upon his shoulders.

They all went upon their way, and Isis said, 'Now let us work a wonder on behalf of these children, so that their father may know who hath sent us unto his house.'

Royal crowns were fashioned and concealed in the measure of barley which had been given them. Then the deities caused a great storm to arise, and in the midst of it they returned to the dwelling of the high priest, and they put the barley in a cellar, and sealed it, saying they would return again and take it away.

It came to pass that after fourteen days Rud–dedit bade her servant to bring barley from the cellar so that beer might be made.

The girl said, 'There is none left save the measure which was given unto the dancing girls.'

'Bring that then,' said Rud–dedit, 'and when the dancing girls return I will give them its value.'

When the servant entered the cellar she heard the low sounds of sweet music and dancing and song. She went and told her mistress of this wonder, and Rud–dedit entered the cellar, and at first could not discover whence the mysterious sounds issued forth. At length she placed

her ear against the sack which contained the barley
given to the dancing girls, and found that the music was
within it. She at once placed the sack in a chest and
locked it, and then told her husband, and they rejoiced
together.

Now it happened that one day Rud-dedit was angry
with her servant, and smote her heavily. The girl vowed
that she would be avenged and said, 'Her three children
will become kings. I will inform King Khufu of this
matter.'

So the servant went away and visited her uncle, who
was her mother's eldest brother. Unto him she told all
that had happened and all she knew regarding the children of her mistress.

He was angry with her and spoke, saying, 'Why come
to me with this secret? I cannot consent to make it
known as you desire.'

Then he struck the girl, who went afterwards to draw
water from the Nile. On the bank a crocodile seized
her, and she was devoured.

The man then went towards the dwelling of Rud-dedit
and he found her mourning with her head upon her
knees. He spoke, saying, 'Why is your heart full of
gloom?'

Rud-dedit answered him, 'Because my servant girl
went away to reveal my secret.'

The man bowed and said, 'Behold! she came unto me and told me all things. But I struck her, and she went towards the river and was seized by a crocodile.'

So was the danger averted. Nor did King Khufu ever discover the babes regarding whom Dedi had prophesied. In time they sat upon the throne of Egypt.

A folk tale regarding the king who reigned in Egypt before Khufu was related by a priest to Herodotus, the Greek historian.

The monarch was called Rhampsinitus. He built the western portion of the temple of Ptah. He also erected two statues--one to Summer, which faced the north, and was worshipped, and the other to Winter, which faced the south, but was never honored. The king possessed great wealth, and he caused to be constructed beside the palace a strong stone chamber in which he kept his riches. One of the builders, however, contrived to place a stone in such a manner that it could be removed from the outside.

It chanced that, after the king had deposited his treasure in the chamber, this builder was stricken with illness and knew his end was nigh. He had two sons, and he told them his secret regarding the stone, and gave them the measurements so that they might locate it.

After the man died, the sons went forth in the darkness of night, and when they found the stone, they removed it. Then they entered the chamber and carried away much treasure, and ere they departed, they closed up the wall again.

The king marveled greatly when he discovered that his riches had been plundered, for the seals of the door were unbroken, and he knew not whom to suspect. Again and again, the robbers returned, and the treasure diminished greatly. At length, the king caused traps to be laid in the chamber, for his guards, who kept watch at the entrances, were unable to prevent the mysterious robberies.

Soon after the brothers returned. They removed the stone, and one of them entered stealthily. He went towards the treasure, as was his custom, but was suddenly caught in a trap. In a moment he realized that escape was impossible, and he reflected that he would be put to death on the morrow, while his brother would be seized and similarly punished. So he said to himself, 'I alone will die.'

When he had thus resolved to save his brother, he called to him softly in the darkness, bidding him to enter cautiously. He made known his great misfortune, and said, 'I cannot escape, nor dare you tarry long lest you be discovered, When they find me here I will be recognized, and they will seize you and put you to death. Cut off my head at once, so that they may not know who I am, and thus save your own life.'

With a sad heart the brother did as he was desired, and carried away the head. Ere he escaped in the darkness he replaced the stone, and no man saw him.

When morning came the king was more astounded than ever to find a headless body entrapped in the treasure chamber, for the door had not been opened, and yet two men had entered and one had escaped. He commanded that the corpse should be hung on the palace wall, and stationed guards at the place, bidding them to keep strict watch, so that they might discover if anyone came to sorrow for the dead man. But no one came nigh.

Meanwhile, the mother grieved in secret. Her heart was filled with anger because the body was exposed in such a manner, and she threatened to inform the king regarding all that had happened if her other son would not contrive to carry away the corpse. The young man attempted to dissuade her, but she only repeated her threat, and that firmly. He, therefore, made preparations to obtain possession of the corpse.

He hired several asses, and on their backs, he put many skins of wine. In the evening, he drove them towards the palace. When he drew near to the guards who kept watch over his brother's body, he removed the stoppers of some of the skins. The wine ran forth upon the highway, and he began to lament aloud and beat his head as if he were in sore distress. The soldiers ran towards the asses and seized them, and caught the wine in vessels, claiming it for themselves. At first, the brother pre-tended to be angry and abused the men; but when they had pacified him, as they thought, he spoke to them pleasantly and began to make secure the stoppers of all the skins.

In a short time, he was chatting with the guards and pretended to be much amused when they bantered him over the accident. Then he invited them to drink, and they filled their flasks readily. So they began, and the young man poured out wine until they were all made very drunk. When they fell asleep, the cunning fellow took down his brother's body, and laid it upon the back of one of the asses. Ere he went away he shaved the right cheeks of the soldiers. His mother welcomed him on his return in the darkness and was well pleased.

The king was very angry when he discovered how the robber had tricked the guards, but he was still deter-mined to have him taken. He sent forth his daughter in disguise, and she waited for the criminal. She spoke to several men, and at length she found him, because he came to know that he was sought and desired to deal cunningly with her. So he addressed her, and she offered to be his bride if he would tell her the most artful thing and also the most wicked thing he had ever done.

He answered readily, 'The most wicked thing I ever did was to cut off my brother's head when he was caught in a trap in the royal treasure chamber, and the most artful was to deceive the king's guards and carry away the body.'

The princess tried to seize him, but he thrust forth his brother's arm, which he carried under his robe, and when she clutched it he made speedy escape.

Great was then the astonishment of the king at the cunning and daring of the robber. He caused a proclamation to be made, offering him a free pardon and a generous reward if he would appear at the palace before him. The man went readily, and His Majesty was so delighted with his speeches and great ingenuity that he gave him his daughter in marriage. There are no more artful people than the Egyptians, but this man had no land equal.

It was told that this same king journeyed to the land of Death, where he played dice with the goddess Isis and now won and now lost. She gave him a napkin embroidered with gold, and on his return, a great festival was held, and it was repeated every year thereafter. On such occasions, it was customary to blindfold a priest and lead him to Isis's temple, where he was left alone. It was believed that two wolves met him and conducted him back to the spot where he was found. The Egyptians esteemed Isis and Osiris as the greatest deities of the underworld."

Chapter 19: Se-Osiris and the Sealed Letter

"There have been many tales told in Ancient Egypt about Setna. He was the son of Rameses the Great. Setna was the wisest scribe of all, and he was the one who found and read the Book of Thoth. Tales have also been told about his son Se-Osiris which means the *Gift of Osiris*. Se-Osiris was a wonderful child who, by the age of 12, was the greatest magician that Egypt had ever known.

His most famous exploit began on a day when Rameses sat in the great hall in his palace at Thebes with all his nobles and princes about him, and the Grand Vizer came bustling in looking very shocked and surprised. He prostrated himself before Rameses and cried: 'Life, health, strength be with you, Oh Pharaoh! There has come to your court a rascally Ethiopian who stands seven feet tall and is demanding to speak with you. He says that he is here to prove that the magic we do in Egypt isn't anything compared to the magic they do in Ethiopia.'

'Bid him enter,' commanded the Pharaoh.

Very soon, a large Ethiopian man walked in and stood before the Pharaoh. He bowed before the Pharaoh and said: 'King of Egypt, I have here in my hand a letter that has been sealed to see if any of your magicians, scribes, or priests are able to read what is written in it without breaking the seal. If none of your magicians, scribes, or priests can read it, I will return to Ethiopia and tell my king and all his people how weak the Egyptian's magic is, and you will be the joke on the lips of all men.'

Pharaoh was both troubled and angry when he heard this. He sent for his wise son Setna to be brought to him immediately and told him what had happened. Setna was upset, but he said, 'Oh Pharaoh, my father; life, health, strength be to you! Bid this barbarian go and take his rest. Let him dine, drink, and sleep in the Royal Guest House until your court is assembled next. At that time, I will bring a magician who will show that we who practice the magic art in Egypt are a match for anyone from the lands beyond Kush.'

'Be it so,' answered Pharaoh. The Ethiopian has led away to the hospitable entertainment of the Royal Guest House.

But even though he had spoken so confidently, Setna was troubled. Even though he had read the Book of Thoth, was considered the wisest man in Egypt, and was the most skilled magician, he could not read a letter that had been written on a papyrus scroll and had been rolled up and sealed without breaking the seal and unrolling the letter.

Once he returned to his palace, he laid down on the couch to think. He looked so troubled and pale that his wife came to him, afraid that he had taken ill. She brought with her their son Se-Osiris. When Setna told his troubles to his son and wife, his wife burst into tears, but his son laughed gleefully.

'My son,' said Setna with a puzzled look, 'why do you laugh when I tell you of that which has caused so much concern to Pharaoh and such sorrow to me, your father?'

'I laugh,' answered Se-Osiris, 'because your trouble is no trouble at all but a gift of the gods to bring great glory to Egypt and humble the proud, overbearing King of Ethiopia and his wizards. Cease from your sorrow. I will read the sealed letter.'

Setna sprang up and looked longingly at the small boy who stood so confidently before him.

'You have great powers of magic, I know, my son,' he said. 'But how can I be certain that when we stand before Pharaoh you can indeed read that which is written on a sealed roll of papyrus?'

'Go to your room where your writings are kept,' answered Se-Osiris. 'Choose any papyrus that you like, seal it if it is not sealed already, and I will read it to you without even taking it out of your hand.'

Setna sprang up and fetched a papyrus from his study. And Se-Osiris read what was written on it while his father held it still rolled and sealed with wax.

Next day Pharaoh Rameses summoned his court once more. When all were assembled he bade the Grand Vizer bring the Ethiopian before him with his sealed letter.

Proudly the huge wizard strode into the hall and with hardly a nod to the greatest of all the Pharaohs, he held up the roll of papyrus and cried: 'King of Egype, let your magicians read what is written in this sealed letter or admit that the magic of Ethiopia is greater than the magic of Egypt!'

'Setna, my son,' said Pharaoh, 'You are the greatest magician in Egypt. Would you please answer this insolent barbarian who, if he were not a messenger, I would have beaten with rods.'

'Oh Pharaoh, life, health, strength be to you!' answered Setna. 'Such a dog as this, who has no reverence for the good god Pharaoh Rameses Usima-res, is not worthy to be pitted against a magician full of years and wisdom. But my son Se-Osiris who, at the young age of 12 is skilled enough already in the secret lore to stand against him, shall read his letter.'

There was a murmur throughout the court and a little ripple of laughter as the small boy stepped forward on one side of Pharaoh's throne and came down to the gigantic Ethiopian who stood scowling at the foot of the dais with the sealed letter held up in his right hand.

'Oh Pharaoh, my grandfather, life, health, strength be to you!' said Se-Osiris in a clear voice so that everyone could hear him. 'The sealed roll in the wizard's hand tells the tale of an insult wrought upon one who held the scourge and the crook, one who wore the Double Crown; a Pharaoh of Egypt who sat where you sat 500 years ago.'

'It tells of a king who ruled as today's king rules over the Ethiopians. He sat one day in his marble summer-house beside the river Nile far away to the south. Between the pillars behind him was a trellis of ebony, and it was grown so thickly with sweet–smelling creepers that it seemed like a thick hedge. In the shade behind it, his greatest magicians sat talking together, and the King, listening idly to their words, heard the first say, *In arms, we may not be able to stand against Egypt, but in magic, we are certainly the masters of Pharaoh our overlord and all his people. Why even I could bring great darkness over all the land of Egypt that would last for three days.*'

'*True,*' said another magician. '*I, for example, could bring a blight upon Egypt that would destroy its crops for one season.*'

'So they went on, each telling of the plague that he could bring upon Egypt, until at last the chief magicians of Ethiopia said, '*As for this dog of a Pharaoh who calls himself our overlord, I could bring him here by magic and cause him to be beaten with 500 strokes of the rod before all the people. Yes, I could do this and carry him back to his palace in Egypt all in the space of five hours.'*

'When the King heard this, he summoned the magicians before him, and said to the chief of them, *'Son of Tnahsit, I have heard your words. If you do to the Pharaoh of Egypt even as you have said, I will give you a greater reward than any magician has ever received.'*

'The Son of Tnahsit bowed before him and at once set about his spells. He fashioned a litter and four bearers in was; he chanted words of power over them and he breathed the breath of life into them, and he bade them hasten to Egypt and bring Pharaoh to Ethiopia during the dark hours of the night.'

When he had read so far in the sealed letter, Se-Osiris turned to the Ethiopian and said, 'These words that I have read, are they not written in the sealed roll that you hold in your hands? The answer truly, or may Amen-Ra blast you where you stand!'

The Ethiopian bowed before Se-Osiris and gasped, 'These words are indeed written there, my lord.'

So Se-Osiris continued reading from the sealed letter: 'All happened as the Son of Tnahsit had promised. Pharaoh was lifted from his royal bed at Thebes, carried to Ethiopia, beaten in public by the King's servants with 500 strokes, and taken back again all in the space of five hours. The next morning he woke in great pain, and the marks of the rods on his back told him that it had been no dream.'

'So Pharaoh summoned his court and called his magicians before him and told them of the shame that had been wrought.'

'I desire vengeance upon the King of Ethiopia,' he declared, 'a vengeance upon his magicians. Moreover, I wish the land of Egypt and the divine person of her Pharaoh to be protected against these barbarians and their evil and insulting magic.'

'Then Pharaoh's Chief Magician, the Kherheb of Egypt, bowed low before him, crying, *'Oh Pharaoh, life, health, strength be to you! It cannot be that this wickedness of the sons of Set who dwell in Nubia and Ethiopia shall continue against your divind majesty. Tonight I shall seek counsel of Thoth, the god of wisdom and magic, in his great temple; and tomorrow be sure, I shall have a charm that will bring both vengeance and protection.'*

'So the Kherheb slept in the temple that night, and Thoth with the ibis-head came and stood over his bed and instructed him in all that was to be done for the honor of Egypt and the protection of the good god her Pharaoh.'

'No Ethiopian litter-bearers visited the Royal Palace that night, but the next night they came again to carry

Pharaoh to Ethiopia to be beaten before all the barbarians. But the magic that Thoth the wise had taught to the Kherheb of Egypt was so strong that their magic was in vain. They could only stand and gibber in the royal bed changer; they could not so much as raise their arms to life Pharaoh on to the magic litter. And presently, they faded away and were no more seen in Egypt.'

'But the next morning, when the Kherheb heard of what had happened in Pharaoh's bed-chamber, he rejoiced exceedingly. And straightway, he set about preparing a magic litter of his own, with four bearers who that night carried the King of Ethiopia into the great square before the Temple of Amen-Ra at Thebes and had him beaten with 500 strokes of the rod before all the people that were assembled.'

'In the morning, the King of Ethiopia woke in his palace sore and troubled. At once, he sent for the Son of Tnahsit and bade him find the magic to protect him against the magicians of Egypt and bring vengeance upon Pharaoh.'

'But the Son of Tnahsit could do nothing. Three times the King of Ethiopia was carried to Thebes and beaten before all the people. Then he humbled himself before the glory of the good god Pharaoh and was beaten no more. But he caused the Son of Tnahsit to be cast out of his palace with many curses, saying, *In life and in death may you wander the earth until you bring venge-*

ance upon Egypt, upon her Pharaoh and upon her magicians and until you prove that there is magic greater than the magic of the magician of Khem.'

Then Se-Osiris pointed to the sealed letter, saying, 'Ethiopian, these words which I have read, are they not written in the roll of papyrus which you hold, still sealed in your hands? The answer truly, or may Amen-Ra blast you where you stand!'

The Ethiopian fell upon his knees and cried, 'These words are indeed written there, mighty magician!'

Then the seal was broken and the letter was written out loud before Pharaoh and all his court. And the words of that letter were the words that Se-Osiris the wonderful child had read. Only in the reading, he paid due honor to the Pharaoh and had spoken of Ethiopia's barbarians in such terms that were proper.

After this, the Ethiopian humbly said, 'Mighty Pharaoh, Lord of Egypt and overlord of Ethiopia, may I go hence in peace?'

But Se-Osiris spoke quickly, saying, 'Oh, Pharaoh, life, health, strength be to you! The wizard who kneels before you has within him the Ba of the Son of Tnahsit. Yes, he is the wizard who wrought such shame upon the Pharaoh who sat upon the throne of the Two Lands and held the scourge and the crook 500 years ago. Is it not right that the battle between the magic of Ethiopia and the magic of Egypt should be fought out to the finish here and now before your eyes?'

Pharaoh Rameses the Great nodded his head and touched his grandson, the wonderful child Se-Osiris with his scepter, saying, 'Kherheb of today, finish that which the Kherbed of five centuries ago began.'

Then to the giant Ethiopian cried, 'Black dog of the south, if you have the magic to match against the magic of Egypt, show it now!'

The Ethiopian laughed grimly. 'White dog of the north,' he cried. 'I defy you! I have such magic at my command that presently Set will take you as his own, and Apep, the Devourer of Souls, will soon be feasting up the Ba of that which was once a Pharaoh of Egypt... Behold!'

The Ethiopian waved the sealed roll as if it had been a wand and pointed to the floor in front of Pharaoh, muttering a great word of power.

At once, there reared up a mighty serpent hissing loudly, its forked tongue flickering evilly and its poisoned fangs bared to kill.

Pharaoh cowered back with a cry. But Se-Osiris laughed merrily, and as he raised his hand, the giant cobra dwindled into a little white worm which he picked up between his thumb and first finger and threw it out the window.

The Ethiopian uttered a howl of rage and waved his arms, spitting curses mingled with incantations as he did. At once a cloud of darkness descended upon the great hall. It turned as black as midnight in the tomb and as dense as the smoke of bodies burning.

But Se-Osiris laughed again. Then he took the darkness in his hands, crushed it together until it was not bigger than a ball like the children would make out of the dark clay beside the Nile, and tossed it out of the window.

A third time the Ethiopian waved his arms, and this time he yelled as if the jaws of Apep had already closed upon him. At once, a great sheet of fierce flame leaped up from the floor and moved forward as if to consume the Pharaoh and all who stood beside him on the royal dais.

But Se-Osiris laughed for the third time. Then he blew upon the sheet of flame, and it drew back and wrapped itself about the Ethiopian. There was one great cry, and then the flame dwindled and went out like a candle when all the wax is burnt away.

On the floor in front of Pharaoh lay only a little pile of ash, and Se-Osiris said quietly, 'Farewell to the Son Tnahsit! May his Ba dwell elsewhere forever, and come not again to trouble Egypt or insult the good god Pharaoh life, health, and strength be to him!'"

Chapter 20:
The Land of The Dead

"There was a visit to the Duat that was recorded and remains today. It was visited by Se-Osiris, who was the wonderful child magician that was able to read the sealed letter, and his father Setna, who was the son of Rameses the Great, a Pharaoh of Egypt.

Setna and Se-Osiris were standing at a window of the palace located at Thebes, watching two funerals making their way to the West. The first funeral was of a rich man. Him mummy had been enclosed in a wooden coffin that had been inlaid with gold. He had many mourners and servants that was carrying him to his burial place. They were carrying gifts for his tomb. Many priests were walking in front and behind him chanting hymns to the gods and reciting all the words and great names of power that he would need on his journey through the Duat.

The second funeral was one of a poor person who had been a laborer his whole life. His two sons were carrying his simple wooden coffin. His widow and daughters-in-law were his only mourners.

'Well,' said Setna, watching the two funerals going down to where the boats were waiting to carry them across the Nile, 'I hope that my fate will be that of the rich noble and not of the poor laborer.'

'On the contrary,' said Se-Osiris, 'I pray that the poor man's fate may be yours and not that of the rich man!'

Setna was hurt very much by his son's words, but Se-Osiris tried to explain them by saying, 'Whatever you may have seen here matters little compared with what will happen to these two in the Judgment Hall of Osiris. I will prove it to you if you trust yourself to me. I know the words of power that open all gates: I can release your Ba and mine. Our souls can then fly into the Duat, the world of the dead, and see what is happening there. Then you will see how different the fates will be of this rich man who worked evil throughout his life, and this poor man who has done nothing but good.'

Setna had learned to believe anything his wonderful child said without surprise, and now he agreed to accompany his son into the Duat, even though he knew that such an expedition would be dangerous: for once there they might not be able to return.

So Setna and Se-Osiris made their way into the sanctuary of the Temple of Osiris where, as members of the royal family, they had power to go.

When Setna had barred the doors, Se-Osiris drew a magic circle around them, around Osiris's statue, and around the altar on which a small cedar fire was burning. Then he threw a specific powder into the flame that was upon the altar. He threw the powder three times, and as he threw it, a ball of fire would rise from the altar and would float away. He then spoke a spell and ended with a great name of power. When this word was spoken, the entire temple rocked, and the flame upon the altar leaped higher, and then it sank into darkness.

But inside the Temple of Osiris wasn't dark. Setna turned to see where the light was coming from. He would have cried out in terror if the silence hadn't pressed on him like a weight that held him paralyzed.

Because standing on either side of the altar, he saw himself and his son Se-Osiris. All of a sudden, he knew that it wasn't just his body and his boy's body for these two bodies lay in the shadows that had been cast by these two forms. The forms were their Kas. Above each of these, Kas hovered a flame that was their spirit or Khou. The clear light of the Khou served to show its Ka and the dim form of the body from which Ka and Khou were drawn.

The silence was then broken by a soft whisper like that of a feather falling but it seemed to fill the entire Temple with sound: 'Follow me now, my father,' said the voice of Se-Osiris, 'for the time is short and we must be back before the morning if we would live to see the Sun of Ra rise again over Egypt.'

Setna turned, and saw beside him the Ba or soul of Se-Osiris. It was a great bird that had golden feathers but it had the head of his son.

'I follow,' he forced his lips to answer. Then as the whisper filled the Temple, he used the golden wings of his Ba to rise and followed the Ba of Se-Osiris.

The roof of the temple seemed to open to let them through, and a moment later they were speeding into the West swifter than an arrow from an Ethiopian's bow.

Darkness lay heavy over Egypt, but one red gash of sunset shone through the great pass in the mountains of the Western Desert, the Gap of Abydos. Through this they sped into the First Region of the Night and saw beneath them the Mesektet Boat in which Ra began his journey into the Duat with the ending of each day. The Boat was splendid. Its trimmings were exquisite. It had the colors of lapis lazuli, turquoise, jasper, emerald, amethyst, and a deep golden glow. A company of gods drew the Boat along the River of Death with golden ropes. Duat's portals were thrown open, and they entered the First Region between the six serpents who were curled on either side. Inside the great Boat of Ra journeyed the Kas of all those who had died that day and were on their way to the Judgment Hall of Osiris.

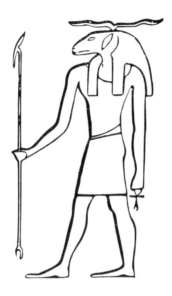

So the Boat moved on its way through regions of night, thick darkness, and they came to the portal of the Second Region. The walls were tall on both sides, and on the top were the points of spears so nobody could climb over. The huge wooden doors turned on pivots, and they also had snakes that breathed poison and fire to guard them. But everyone who passed through on the Boat of Ra and spoke the words of power that had been set aside for that portal, were able to make the doors swing open.

The Second Region was the Kingdom of Ra, and the heroes and gods of old who had lived on earth when he was King dwelt there in peace and happiness, guarded by the Spirits of the Corn who make the wheat and barley flourish and cause the fruits of the earth to increase.

Yet not one of the dead who voyaged in the Boat of Ra might pause there or set foot on the land because they had to pass into Amenti, which was the Third Region of the Duat where the Judgment Hall of Osiris stood waiting to receive them.

So the Boat came to the next portals, and at the word of power the great wooden doors screamed open on their pivots but not so loudly did they scream as the man who lay with one of the pivots turning in his eye as punishment for all the evil he had done while he was alive.

Into the Third Region sailed the Boat of Ra, and here the dead disembarked in the outer court of the judgement Hall of Osiris. But the Boat itself continued on its way through the nine other Regions of the Night until the rebirth of Ra from out of the mouth of the Dragon of the East brought dawn once more upon the earth and the rising of the sun. Yet the sun would not rise unless each night Ra fought and defeated the Dragon Apep, who seeks to devour Ra in the Tenth Region of the Night.

The Ba of Setna and Se-Osiris did not follow the Boat of Ra further, but flew over the Kas of the newly dead who came one by one to the portal of the Hall of Osiris and one by one were challenged by the Door Keeper.

'Stay!' cried the Door Keeper. 'I will not announce thee unless you know my name!'

'Understander of Hearts is your name,' answered each instructed Ka. 'Searcher of Bodies is your name!'

'Then to whom should I announce thee?' asked the Door Keeper.

'Thou should tell of my coming to the Interpreter of the Two Lands.'

'Who then is the Interpreter of the Two Lands?'

'It is Thoth the Wise God.'

So each Ka passed through the doorway and in the Hall Thoth was waiting to receive him, saying: 'Come with me. Yet why hast thou come?'

'I have come here to be announced,' answered the Ka.

'What is thy condition?'

'I am pure of sin.'

'Then to whom shall I announce thee? Shall I announce thee to him whose ceiling is of fire, whose walls are living serpents, whose pavement is water?'

'Yes,' answered the Ka, 'announce me to him, for he is Osiris.'

So ibis-headed Thogh led the Ka to where Osiris sat upon his throne, wrapped in the mummy clothes of the dead, wearing the uraeus crown upon his forehead and holding the scourge and the crook crossed upon his breast in front of him stood a huge balance with two scales. Then the jackal-headed Anubis, who is the god of death, stepped forward to lead the Ka to the judgment.

But before the Weighing of the Heart, every dead man's Ka spoke in his own defense, saying: 'I am pure! I am pure! I am pure! I am pure! My purity is as that of the Bennu bird, the bright Phoenix whose nest is upon the stone persea-tree, the obelisk at Heliopolis. Behold me, I have come to you without sin, without guilt, without evil, without a witness against me, without one against whom I have taken action. I live on truth, and I eat of truth. I have done that which men said and that with which gods are content. I have satisfied each god with that which he desires. I have given bread to the hungry, water to the thirsty, clothing to the naked, and a boat to him who could not cross the River. I have provided offerings to the gods and offerings to the dead. So preserve me from Apep, the Eater-up of Souls, so protect me Lord of the Atef Crown, Lord of Breath, the great god Osiris.'

Then came the moment which the evildoer feared but the good man welcomed with joy.

Anubis took the heart out of the Ka that was the double of his earthly body and placed it on the Scale, and on the other side of the scale, he placed the Feather of Truth. Heavy was the heart of the rich man, and it pushed the Scale down. Lower and lower it sank, while Thoth marked the angle of the beam until the Scale sank so low that Ammit the Devourer of Hearts could catch the rich man's heart in his jaws and bear it away. Then the rich man was driven forth into the thick darkness of the Duat to dwell with Apep the Terrible in the Pits of Fire.

When Anubis placed the poor man's heart onto the scale along with the Feather of Truth, the Feather sank down, and his heart rose up. Thoth cried aloud to Osiris and the gods, 'True and accurate are the words this man has spoken. He has not sinned; he has not done evil towards us. Let not the Eater up of Souls have power over him. Grant that the eternal bread of Osiris be given to him, and a place in the Fields of Peace with the followers of Horus!'

Then Horus took the dead man by the hand and led him before Osiris, saying, 'I have come to thee, oh Unnefer Osiris, bringing with me this new Osiris. His heart was true at the coming forth from the Balance. He has not sinned against any god or any goddess. Thoth has weighed his heart and found it true and righteous. Grant that there may be given to him the bread and beer of Osiris; may he be like the followers of Horus!'

The Osiris inclined his head, and the poor man passed rejoicing into the Fields of Peace there to dwell, taking joy in all the things he had loved best in life, in a rich land of plenty, until Osiris returned to earth, taking with him all those who had proved worthy to live forever as his subjects.

All these things and more the Ba of Se-Osiris showed to the Ba of his father Setna; and at length, he said, 'Now you know why I wished your fate to be that of the poor man and not of the rich man. For the rich man was he in whose eye the pivot of the Third Door was turning, but the poor man is dwelling forever in the Fields of Peace, clad in fine robes and owning all the offerings which accompanied the evil rich man to his tomb.'

Then the two Ba spread their golden wings and flew back through the night to Thebes. There they went back into their bodies which their Kas had been guarding in the Temple of Osiris, and were able to return to their place as ordinary, living father and child, in time to see the sunrise beyond the Eastern desert and turn the cliffs of Western Thebes to pink and purple and gold as a new day dawned over Egypt."

Chapter 21: The Treasure Thief

"Rameses the Third was the Pharaoh who, when he first came to be Pharaoh wanted to marry Helen of Troy. He ruled for many years, and Egypt grew very prosperous under him. Early on during his reign, he defeated invasions from both Libya and Palestine. After all this, he lived at peace with his neighbors and encouraged trading to such an extent that he became the richest of all the Pharaohs.

Rameses gathered his treasures together in the form of gold and silver and precious stones. The more he gathered, the more anxious he became for fear that anybody would steal his treasures.

He sent for his Master Builder, Horemheb, to come to him, 'Build me a mighty treasure house of the hewn stone of Syene; make the floor of solid rock and the walls so thick that no man may pick a hole in them, and rear high the roof with stone into a tall pyramid so that no entrance may be broken through that either.'

Then Horemheb, the Master Builder, kissed the ground before Rameses and cried, 'Oh Pharaoh! Life, health, strength be to you! I will build such a treasure house for you as the world has never seen, nor will any man be able to force a way into it.'

Heremheb set all the stonemasons in the land of Egypt to work day and night quarrying and hewing the stone from the hard rock on the edge of the desert above Syene where the Nile falls from its most northerly cataract near the isle of Elephantine. And when the stone was hewn, he caused it to be drawn on sleds down to the Nile and loaded on boats which bore it down to Western Thebes, where the temple of Rameses was already rising, which stands to this day and is now called Madinet Habu.

Under the care of the Master Builder the walls of the new building were reared and a pyramid was built over the whole, leaving a great treasure chamber in the middle. In the entrance, he set sliding doors of stone, and others of iron and bronze. When the untold riches of Pharaoh Rameses were placed in the chamber, the doors were locked, and each was sealed with Pharaoh's great seal, that none might copy on pain of death both here and in the Duat where Osiris reigns.

Yet Horemheb, the Master Builder, played Pharaoh false. In the thick wall of the Treasure House, he made a narrow passage, with a stone at either end turning on a pivot that, when closed, looked and felt like any other part of the smooth, strong wall, except for those who knew where to feel for the hidden spring that held it firmly in place.

Using this secret entrance, Horemheb was able to add to the reward which Pharaoh gave to him when the

Treasure House was complete. Yet he did not add much, for very soon, a great sickness fell upon him, and presently he died.

But on his death bed, he told his two sons about the secret entrance to the Treasure House. When he was dead, and they had buried his body with all honors in a rock chamber among the Tombs of the Nobles at Western Thebes, the two young men made such good use of their knowledge that Pharaoh soon realized that his treasure was beginning to grow mysteriously less and less.

Rameses was at a loss to understand how the thieves got in, for the royal seals were never broken, but get in, they certainly did. Pharaoh as fast becoming a miser, and he paid frequent visits to his Treasure House and knew every object of value in it, and the treasure continued to go.

At last, Pharaoh commanded that cunning traps and meshes should be set near the chests and vessels from which the treasure was disappearing.

This was done secretly, and when next the two brothers made their way into the Treasure House by the secret entrance to collect more gold and jewels, the first to step across the floor towards the chests was caught in one of the traps and knew at once that he could not escape.

So he called out, 'Brother! I am caught in a snare, and all your cunning cannot get me out of it. Probably I shall be dead by the time Pharaoh sends his guards to find out if he has caught the Treasure Thief; if not, he is certain to have me tortured cruelly until I tell all, and then he will put me to death. And whether I live or die, he or one of the royal guards will recognize me, and then they will catch you, and you too will perish miserably and maybe our mother also. I am bound, and if you hope to pass the judgment of Osiris since I am bound, that you draw your sword and strike off my head and carry it away with you. Then I shall die quickly and easily; moreover, no one will recognize my body so that you at least will be safe from Pharaoh's vengeance.'

The second brother tried to break the trap but, at last, realized that it was in vain. He agreed that it was better for one of them to die than both and that if his brother were recognized, their whole family might suffer; he drew his sword and did as he had begged him to do. Then he went back through the passage, closing the stones carefully behind him, and buried his brother's head with all reverence.

When day dawned, Pharaoh came to his Treasure Chamber and was astonished to find the body of a man, naked and headless, held fast in one of his traps. But there was still no sign of a secret entrance, for the Treasure Thief had been careful to remove all tracks while it was quite certain that the seals on the doors had not been broken.

Yet Pharaoh was determined to catch the Treasure Thief. So he gave orders that the body should be hung on the outer wall of the palace and a guard of soldiers stationed nearby to catch anyone who might try to take it away for burial or anyone who came near to weep and lament

When the mother of the dead man heard that the body of her son was hanging on the palace wall and could not be given the sacred rites of burial, she turned upon her second son, crying, 'If the body of your brother remains unburied, his spirit cannot find peace in the Duat not come before Osiris where he sits in judgment. He will instead wander forever as a ghost, lost upon this earth. Therefore you must bring me his body or else I go straight to Pharaoh and beg for it by the love which he bore to your father, Horemheb, his Master Builder. If he learns that you are the Treasure Thief, I cannot help it; but I will at least bury you with your father and brother in the great tomb of Horemheb.'

At first, her son tried to persuade her that the head's burial was enough; because of this, he had set secretly where Horemheb lay. And then he pointed out to her that it was surely better for one of her sons to lie unburied than for both of them to die. But she would not listen to him, and he was forced to promise to do his best to recover his brother's body.

So he disguised himself as an old merchant, loaded two donkeys with skins of wine, and set out along the road which ran by the palace wall.

As he passed the place where the soldiers were encamped, he made the donkeys jostle against each other, and he secretly made holes in the wineskins which had bumped together as if some sharp pieces of metal on their harnesses had done it.

The good red wine ran out onto the ground, and the false merchant wept and lamented loudly, pretending to be so upset that he could not decide which of the skins to save first.

As soon as they saw what was happening, the guard's soldiers came running to help the merchant or rather to help themselves. They proceeded to drink the wine until the two damaged skins were completely emptied, and the wine was hitting their heads.

By this time, the merchant had made friends with his rescuers and was so grateful to them for saving his wine from being wasted on the sand of the desert that he made them a present of another skin of wine and sat down to share it with them. They did not refuse their help when yet another skin was broached, but before it was emptied, they were past saying anything and lay snoring on the ground with their mouths open.

Darkness was falling by this time, and the false merchant had no difficulty in taking down the body of his brother from the wall, wrapping it in empty wineskins, and carrying it away on one of his donkeys. Then, having taken a lock of hair from one side of each soldier's head, he went triumphantly home to his mother, and the funeral was completed before the morning,

When it was light, and Pharaoh discovered that the body was gone, his rage was great, and he caused the guards to be laid out and beaten on their feet with rods as a punishment for their drunkenness.

'Whatever the cost, I must have the Treasure Thief!' cried Pharaoh, and forthwith he invented a new plan to catch him. He disguised one of his own daughters, a royal Princess, as a great lady from a foreign land, and bade her camp before the city gates and offer herself in marriage to the man who could tell her the cleverest and wickedest deed he had done in the whole of his life.

The Treasure Thief guessed at once who the strange maiden was and why she was asking these questions. But he was determined to outdo Pharaoh in cunning. So he went to visit the Princess just as the sun was sinking, he carried with him, hidden under his cloak, the hand, and arm of a man who had lately been executed for treason by command of the Pharaoh.

'Fair Princess, I would win you to be my wife,' he said.

'Then tell me the cleverest and wickedest things that you have ever done,' she answered, 'and I will say yes to your offer of marriage if they are wickeder and cleverer than any I have yet heard.'

As the sun went down behind the Valley of the Kings, the Treasure Thief told his tale to the Princess.

'And so,' he ended, 'the wickedest thing I ever did was to cut off my own brother's head when he was caught in Pharaoh's trap yonder in the secret chamber of the Treasure House; and the cleverest was to steal his body from under the noses of the soldiers who were set to guard it.'

Then the Princess cried out to the royal attendants who were hidden nearby as she seized the thief, saying, 'Come quickly, for this is the man Pharaoh is seeking! Come quickly, for I am holding him by the arm!'

But when Pharaoh's attendants crowded in with their lighted torches and lamps, the Treasure Thief had already slipped away into the darkness, leaving the dead man's arm in the Princess's hands, and she saw how cleverly she had been tricked.

When Pharaoh Rameses heard of this further example of daring and craftiness, he exclaimed, 'This man is too clever to punish. The land of Khem prides itself on excelling the rest of the word in wisdom, but this man has more wisdom than anyone else in the land of Khem! Go, proclaim through the city of Thebes that I will pardon him for all that he has done, and reward him richly if henceforth he will serve me truly and faithfully.'

So, in the end, the Treasure Thief married the Princess and became a loyal servant of Pharaoh Rameses III. Nor did he ever have any further need to enter the Royal Treasure Chamber by the secret entrance made into it by Horemheb, the Master Builder."

Chapter 22: Isis and the
Seven Scorpions

"Anytime Isis left Horus in the evening while they were in hiding in the papyrus swamps near Buto, seven scorpions accompanied her. Three of the scorpions preceded her, Petet, Tjetet, and Matet, to make sure that the path ahead of her was safe. At her side were the scorpions, Mesetet and Mesetetef. Bringing up the rear were Tefen and Befen.

Each night, Isis warned her companions to be extremely cautious as to avoid alerting Set as to where she was. She would remind them not to speak to anyone they met along the way.

One night, Isis was traveling to the Town of the Two Sisters of the Nile Delta. A wealthy noblewoman saw the strange party arrive and quickly shut the door to her house. The scorpions were enraged at her rude behavior and decided to teach the woman a lesson. In preparation, six of the scorpions gave their poisons to Tefen, who loaded his stranger with it. Meanwhile, a humble peasant girl had offered her simple home as a refuge to Isis.

The scorpion's anger was not improved by the young girl's kindness toward their mistress, and Tefen snuck out of the house. He crawled under the door of the noblewoman's house and stung her son. Distraught, the woman wandered through the town seeking help for her child, who was on the verge of death.

Isis heard the woman's cries for help, and even though the woman had been unkind to her, Isis could not bear the thought of the death of an innocent child and left with the woman to help her son. Isis held the boy in her arms and spoke words of great magic. She named each of the scorpions and thereby dominated them, rendering their combined poison to be harmless in the child.

The noblewoman was humbled by Isis's unconditional kindness and offered all of her worldly wealth to Isis and the peasant girls who had shown hospitality to a stranger."

Conclusion

Thank you for making it through to the end of the book. I hope that you have found the book informative as well as entertaining. These myths are timeless and can be enjoyed time and time again. They can also be a source of inspiration if you are planning a trip to Japan. See if you can find some of the real-life inspirations for these stories.

Finally, if you found this book useful in any way, a review on Amazon is always appreciated!

CPSIA information can be obtained
at www.ICGtesting.com
Printed in the USA
LVHW041931230822
726685LV00003B/319

9 781801 131087